JOANNA BLAKE

A NOTE ABOUT THIS BOOK

The main character of this book appears briefly in another novel. Jagger served with Kyle in Go Long and just begged me to write him his own story. They are both stand-alone novels that do not need to be read in any particular order.

This edition contains several excerpts.

Enjoy!

Xoxox,
   Joanna

COCKPIT

She's the one who got away. But I live for the chase...

I'm a thrill seeker. I fly the fastest jets in the world, and ride my motorcycle when I'm on the ground. The only thing that matters to me is speed. Why would I ever think about settling down?

Jenny Reeds, that's why. One look in those hazel eyes and I found a thrill no dogfight could match. For one wild, unforgettable night, she was mine. I wanted to keep her close but she disappeared without even telling me her last name.

I never forgot her.

I did my tour and flew combat missions in desert skies. Now they have me pushing papers and training new pilots. I thought I'd be bored to tears.

Guess who I run into my first night back?

It's her, my wild-eyed, fiery-haired beauty. Turns out she's the General's daughter. But that won't stop me. I'm persistent and it doesn't take too long before she's back in my arms.

Only one problem. She's kept one hell of a secret from me. She had a baby while I was overseas. *My baby.*

Now I want them both under my roof. *Permanently.* She's got other ideas but that won't stop me. I've never failed a mission yet and I don't intend to start now.

Cockpit **is a standalone novel with a guaranteed HEA and no cheating. This edition includes bonus materials and will end before 100%!**

For my most avid reader, my back rubber and dish do-er. I love and appreciate you and your tiny butt every single day.

XOXOX

ACKNOWLEDGMENTS

Special thanks are owed to the people who got me through writing this book.

Thanks to Sabrina, Jordan, Abigail, Vanessa, Sosie, Winter and Chance for encouraging me every step of the way.

Thanks to Jen Wildner for her endless cheerleading, hard work and giving me the name and inspiration for the lead character.

Thank you Jess Peterson for her military fact checking and expertise.

Thank you to my amazing group of readers, the Belles! I couldn't do it without you. Your feedback and support mean the world to me.

And last but not least, extra special thanks to LJ for dealing with my anxiety about zombie pilots with humor, grace and incredible talent.

CREDITS

LJ ANDERSON, MAYHEM COVER DESIGN
JAMES CRITCHLEY, COVER PHOTO
ANDREW ENGLAND, COVER MODEL
JUST ONE MORE PAGE BOOK PROMOTIONS
PINCUSHION PRESS

PROLOGUE

I rolled over, staring at the girl sleeping beside me. She looked like an angel, with her golden red hair spilling over a stunningly beautiful face. Her skin was creamy and kissable. I lifted the blankets, looking at her naked, perfect body.

Her skin was kissable *everywhere.*

I lowered the covers, calculating how much time we had. My departure transit was at zero eight hundred. That was two hours from now. That meant that I had to wake her, if I wanted to have her again.

And I did. Lord have mercy, I did.

In fact, my cock had woken me up to tell me so. Not regular morning wood. This was a Goddamn Redwood. One of those thousand year-old trees big enough to drive a car through. And it had her name written all over it.

"Wake up, sweetheart."

She rubbed her button nose, scrunching up her face like a little girl. A wave of tenderness came over me. All of the sudden, I wished my transit was tomorrow. Or the next day.

Or never.

I had no fear about shipping out, even though the area I was heading to was volatile.

But after last night, I did not want to leave. Not yet. Not until I knew she would be here waiting for me.

The unthinkable had happened.

Derek Jagger, AKA Master Seargant Panty Dropper, had met his match.

And then some.

When I'd walked into the bar off base last night, I'd planned on drinking myself into a stupor, then taking one of the many local girls who'd expressed interest back to my room for the night, and draining my balls until they were dry as dust.

But then I'd laid eyes on her. Young and fresh and pretty, she'd looked out of place in the seedy bar. With her long auburn hair and flashing green eyes, she was classically beautiful. But it was her bombshell body that had men lining up to buy her drinks. I watched as she shot 'em down one by one.

Oh boy, did I watch. It was like my eyeballs were glued to her, watching as she scoffed at the guys who tried to pick her up. She wasn't even nice about it either.

She was feisty as hell. I liked that in a woman. As long as she didn't do it to me.

Good God damn but the woman was a looker! The face of an angel with a body that could turn a grown man to stone with a glance. Long legs, a tiny waist and what could only be described as dangerous curves.

Very, very dangerous.

Of course, the fact that she was dressed like a schoolgirl only made all the dicks in the room harder. She wasn't wearing a uniform or anything like that. Just tight, light colored jeans and a white blouse with tiny flowers on it.

Just a regular, innocent, sexy as hell, every-day look.

It wasn't a stereotypical, schoolgirl outfit with a plaid miniskirt and folded over socks. She literally looked like a good girl, who was going to school. She's just wandered into a dirt bag bar by mistake.

I was no dummy. This little peach was out of her element. Here to cause trouble. Go wilding. Or slumming. I decided right off the bat that I wanted her for myself.

Oh yeah, I was going after her with military precision.

Either way, I was going to make sure she got home safe.

Didn't matter if she said yes or no to me. I was walking her home at the end of her big night out. Hopefully with a little pit stop off at my pad to dip my stick. Scratch that.

A long-ass pit stop.

Instead of slobbering all over her like all the other jokers in the place, I'd challenged her to a game of pool. I'd hoped to impress her with my formidable skills. Instead, I'd lost.

She was damn good at playing pool. A ringer even. The kind who took a guy for all he was worth.

I didn't mind though. She looked damn good racking them up and knocking them down. I loved watching her strutting around the table and bending over to take her shots.

Let's just say I was a little distracted.

After that though, s*he'd* challenged *me* to a game of darts. I'd won that game, but barely. The evening progressed with unrelenting sexual tension and sparring. Beers had turned to shots, and flirting had turned to making out in the parking lot.

When things got too hot and heavy, I brought her back here. We'd screwed like rabbits. The sheets were still damp from our all night fuck-a-thon.

The girl was by far the best lay I'd ever had.

And I was nowhere near satisfied.

"Time to get up, sugar lips."

Her eyes opened and I smiled at her. She blinked at me in confusion and then relaxed. She stretched and the sheets slipped down, uncovering her luscious breasts.

"Hmmm... what time is it?"

I leaned forward, kissing her neck.

"Early. We still have time."

"Time for what?"

"Breakfast in bed. For me anyway."

She gasped as I slid my hand down her body, tugging her hip so that she rolled against me. I kissed her deeply, playing tonsil hockey like a pro. Then I let my fingers get busy, tweaking her nipples for a while before sliding between those silky thighs of hers.

She whimpered as I toyed with her slippery folds. I was ready to get my dick wet. But I wanted to taste her first.

I pressed her onto her back and looked up at her as I kissed my way down her body. Damn, but the girl looked specfuckingtacular from every angle! Especially this one...

I kissed her sweet little pussy, smiling at the high-pitched sounds she made. I ran my fingers through her neatly trimmed bush. It was bright red and sexy as hell.

Then I got down to work.

I worked her clit into my mouth as I used my fingers to open her. The girl was tight and I was extremely well-endowed. She needed to be warmed up before I sunk my torpedo.

She cried out, arching her back as I felt her flutter around me.

Hell yes, that was nice. I felt like the pussy eatin' champ of the world. I made sure she was done coming before I shifted up, grabbing a condom to quickly wrap my dick.

I held my cock against her pussy and slowly slid in. I grunted at the sensation. Her puffy little lips gripped me, almost sucking me in.

"Hmmffff... Jesus, you feel good."

It didn't just feel good. It almost felt *too* good. I'd never felt anything like it. Not sex. Not a blowjob. Not my own damn hand. Not blowing bad guys out of the sky.

This was pretty much paradise.

My balls felt like lead weights as I started to ride her. They were bombs, ready to go off. I grimaced, trying to hold back.

Easy does it Jagger... I wanted to make this last. I knew it was the last time I was getting laid for a long ass time. Besides, she was one in a million. I wanted to remember this when I was laying alone in my bunk in the middle of some God forsaken desert.

Her gorgeous thighs lifted up and wrapped around me.

"Oh! Jagger..."

I moaned. Her hot little pussy was clamping down on me like a vice. It was too much. I was going to pop.

I reached down to strum her clit as my strokes got out of tempo and jerky. I wanted her to come with me. I wanted us to ride the fucktastic rainbow together.

"Oh FUCK!"

I felt her coming as the seed ripped out of my body. It was an explosion of pleasure, so

14

intense it almost hurt. I'd never come like that in my life.

Considering how much I'd fucked and drank the night before, it was a Goddamn miracle.

She was whimpering, squealing like a dolphin as I thrust into her wildly. Then I stopped, my shoulders shaking, still balls deep inside her. It was the sweetest thing I'd felt in my whole damn life.

I stared down at her. My hands were shaking. I was shocked by the force of my orgasm. She looked dazed too, her face flushed and sweaty. I leaned down to kiss her, feeling the urge to say love words rising to my lips.

I kept my damn mouth shut though. No need to make an ass of myself and scare her off. Instead I grinned, rolling to the side.

There was plenty of time for making an ass of myself later.

I reached down to pull the condom off my shaft and froze. My hand touched bare cock. I was soaked with our juices.

Our juices.

"Oh shit."

The condom must have broke. I looked at her, sprawled on the bed like a fallen angel. I would tell her. But not until we cleaned up.

No need to spoil her afterglow.

I pulled the rubber from around the base of my cock and threw it away. I poured her a glass of water, holding it while she took a sip. Then I drank the rest of it down.

Fucking like that was thirsty work.

But damn if I didn't like the job.

She smiled at me.

"I'm all sticky."

I smiled and stood up.

"Better get you washed up."

I carried her into the bathroom and set her on her feet. I turned on the water, making sure it was good and hot. I stepped into the shower, reaching for her. She froze, a look of horror flashing over her face.

"Wait- what time is it?"

"Zero seven thirty."

Her face paled, a look of horror washing over it.

"He's going to kill me!"

She ran out of the place, grabbing clothes as she went. I chased her out the door, barely wrapped in my towel.

"Wait, Jenny! Where are you going?"

She shouted *'later Jagger!'* as she ran breakneck down the road, soldiers jumping out of her way. I ran after her but she was already lost in the crowd.

I stood there, barefoot and bare-assed, wondering how the hell I'd let her get away from me. I'd had plans for her. Big plans.

Guys were catcalling me as I clutched the towel over my package. I cursed and turned around, my ass bare to the world. She'd gotten away. Now I'd never fucking find her.

I was feeling a full on case of the blues as I went back to my room to get ready to ship out. I was clean and showered, pulling on my fatigues when I noticed it.

Blood.

The sheets were red with it. But only at the base of the bed where I'd taken her the first time. It couldn't have been her lady time, I would have noticed it.

Lord knows I'd gone down on her enough in the past eight hours or so.

I was scratching my head when it came to me.

My sweet, feisty little angel had been a virgin.

I cursed, running my hands through my hair. I wasn't surprised. I'd had one hell of a time getting inside her the first time, even though she'd been more than ready for me.

She'd given me her virginity. That had to mean something. I wanted more though. I wanted this girl to be mine.

Unfortunately, I was shit out of luck.

I knew I would never find her now, even though I would give it a try. I'd even call my buddies in intelligence. But it was a long shot for sure. All I had was her first name. And it was the most common name in the world.

Jenny.

1
JAGGER

Marines from all over the camp crowded around me as I dug into my trunk. My unit was going home, so I was giving my goodies away along with the rest of the guys. All the stuff that made living in the ass end of the world bearable.

Skin mags. Smokes. Booze. A couple of dog-earred paperback novels. An unopened bag of socks my foster sister had sent. Dice.

I even had a set of checkers.

I was keeping my lucky deck of cards though.

"And to you K-Dawg, I bequeath my prized possession. Racy redheads."

I made a big show of handing Ken the magazine that had gotten me through a lot of lonely nights. I had a thing for redheads now. Ever since her.

The fallen angel.

Sweet Jenny, whatever her last name was.

The picture I liked the best was one of a girl from the back. All you could see was her red hair and the curve of her ass. It almost looked like her. The one that had got away. It was a damn shame too.

I'd thought about her the whole damn time I was overseas. I was tempted to go back to that base and try and track her down, even though it was two states away from my next assignment.

I'd look like an idiot walking into a bar and asking about a girl with no last name that I'd met a year and a half ago.

Fuck though, after the night we'd had it might be worth it.

"Do I need gloves for this? Or maybe a hazmat suit?"

"No K-Dawg. I jack off into a condom."

"What the fuck for?"

"Reminds me of the real thing dude."

I reached into my trunk and pulled out a roll of rubbers.

"Speaking of which."

I tossed them into the crowd. The guys grabbed at them, acting like lunatics. Not that many of them were going to get laid over here. They'd probably end up making balloon animals out of them. But I knew they had to let off steam anyway they could.

Hell, I did too.

Gambling, running laps around the perimeter of the encampment, or just thinking about what I was going to do when I got back to the states.

This time it was for good. My unit was being sent back. But I was going to be a pilot trainer for the duration of my service. For some reason, the powers that be had thought I would be good at it.

It would be a big change, but I was ready for it.

Truth be told, I was tired.

"I'm going to miss you fuckers."

It was true. That was the only hard thing about this. My unit was going home, but I had other friends here. Leaving these guys to face God knows what without me felt like I was cutting off a hand with a rusty saw.

Still, not getting shot at was going to be a nice change of pace.

Not that I was going to do what everybody else did. I'd seen it time and again. Single guys left and then the next thing you knew, they were popping out babies left and right. Even Joss had done it. The iceman himself had fallen in love with a pop star of all things, gotten hitched and started procreating.

If he could crack under pressure, then the rest of these guys were toast. They might as well start picking out tablecloths. I, on the other hand, had things to do.

Manly things. Things with women. With hard drinking. With my bike.

I wanted to ride cross-country, hitting every juke joint I came across. I got a little misty eyed thinking about it.

Hell, maybe I'd even find my little redhead.

JENNY

"Oh GOD!"

I shook my hand, staring at it. It was covered in poop. Hallie had the runs again. And she hadn't started to go until I had her diaper off.

"Hallie!!!"

She just looked up at me and cooed. I wanted to kiss her when she did that. All these feelings rushed into me. Love. Fear. Pride.

Every damn time.

Of course, I had to get the poop off both of us first.

I lifted my daughter and held her up while I wiped down her chubby little legs and ass. I turned her slightly and sighed. Some poop had managed to get all the way up her back.

"How'd you do that, you little poop machine?"

She made a soft sound that sounded like a laugh. Babies weren't supposed to laugh but I would swear, mine did. She had a very sophisticated sense of humor too.

Mostly, she liked laughing at her mama.

I got her cleaned up and leaned her against me as I bundled the used diaper up and threw it away. Then I wiped down the changing table and put a fresh diaper down.

I sniffed her neck, unable to resist the impulse. She smelled sweet, even after her loose stools. I had to hope she wouldn't have another explosive poop while I was gone. I needed to go out for a few hours and that meant having dad watch the baby.

The General did not do well with poop.

But since I didn't have money for a babysitter, he was going to have to do it. He never complained when I left Hallie with him, but I could feel his disapproval. He had been shocked when I'd canceled college because I was pregnant. He'd been hurt and angry and upset.

But he never showed it in front of his granddaughter, who he adored.

Just... not her poop.

I sighed, setting her down in her bouncy chair. I had the basics to take care of her. I should be grateful. My Gran had sent an absurd amount of baby stuff. And dad gave me money to shop at the grocery store on base.

We were covered.

But it wasn't enough. I had plans. Big plans. I wanted my independence. I needed to move out if I was ever going to get my freedom.

And I needed money to do it.

Basically, what I needed was a job.

And today, I was going to go get one.

2
JAGGER

I dropped my bags and checked out my housing. As a single man, I didn't qualify for a house. Instead it was more like a condo.

A bare bones, boxy, condo that hadn't been renovated since the 90's from the looks of it.

But it was mine.

The housing was townhouse style, with two levels and a small patio out back. Even had a front porch with an ancient rocking chair someone had left behind. Looked like a good place to have a cigar and a cold one on a hot night.

After camping out in the desert with a bunch of sweaty guys and communal showers, I definitely was not complaining.

I grinned, opening some windows to air the place out.

The fridge was empty. The cupboards were bare. The bed was unmade.

I would have to buy everything, even silverware and dishes. But that was okay. That could wait. At the moment all I wanted a hot shower, a cold beer and a hot meal.

And something to look at. A girl maybe. Though I doubted I'd find anyone to compare to *her*.

I shook it off. Let it go, Jagger. She's gone.

She clearly didn't want to be found either. It's not like she didn't know my name after all. There weren't too many fixed-wing pilots named Jagger.

There weren't any other active service Marines with that name, period. As far as I knew anyway.

It still stung man. It really did. She could have tracked me down. Lots of girls liked writing to guys stationed overseas, even if it didn't mean a damn thing in the long run.

It was the patriotic thing to do.

They knew how rough it was and they did it. Some of them even liked doing it. After a while though, lots of girls moved on. I was sure that was what had happened.

Sexy little ex-virginal Jenny had moved on.

I needed to stop thinking about her. About that night. Going out would be a step in the right direction. So without even unpacking, I stepped out in some clean civilian wear.

I'd heard there was joint with the best ribs this side of the Mississippi.

It was just off base, there almost exclusively for the military. There were some locals too of course, but like most bases, we were deliberately out in the middle of nowhere. So, the pickin's were slim in the women department.

That was alright though. I wanted to eat and drink until I passed out. I pushed open the swinging wooden door and stopped cold in my tracks.

I could not believe my eyes.

My angel was behind the counter, wiping down the bar.

I felt love whallopped, then and there. What were the chances? It was one in a million, if not more that I'd find her again. And on my first damn day back.

It was a sign. It had to be.

I stood there, counting every damn lucky star in the whole damn sky. And then a healthy dose of anger crept in. She'd blown me off and here she was, looking every bit as beautiful as I remembered.

More beautiful, if that was even possible.

Her face looked thinner now, as if she'd lost some of her baby fat. She'd been so young the last time I saw her. She straightened up and I inhaled sharply.

She'd filled out too. And that was saying something, considering the God given gifts she'd had before. Damn straight, she'd been blessed in the curves department. And then some.

The woman was stacked.

Everywhere.

I realized I was standing in the open doorway like an idiot and walked the rest of the way in. There was a spring in my step that hadn't been there in a long ass time. I found a table in the back, hoping she'd come and take my order. I had to figure out what I was going to say to her.

Because I wanted that woman in my bed again.

Tonight.

Oh yeah, this was going to be one hell of a homecoming.

JENNY

I wrung out the rag, shaking my hands to dry them. This job was hell on the fingernails. But I'd already made more money in tips than I'd seen in a lifetime full of strict allowance and babysitting on all the bases we'd lived on.

Some of the guys knew who I was of course. That helped them open their wallets. But I think the rest were just starved for female company.

I sighed.

I was pretty starved for company myself.

Too bad Jagger hadn't turned out to be the Prince Charming I'd thought he was. He'd shown me one hell of a good time that night. He'd impressed me and left me wanting more.

But I'd asked around about him after he shipped out. Especially after I found out I was carrying his baby.

What I found out kept me from trying to get in touch.

I shouldn't have been surprised. But I was. The way he had treated me that night... he had been so tender and passionate.

He hadn't seemed like a manwhore.

According to rumour though, he was. The biggest player in the Marines apparently. Maybe the entire Armed Forces.

That had stung a bit, knowing I was one of many. Many-many. Not just dozens of women.

Hundreds of women.

But I'd picked myself up. So what if my first time had been with a he-slut? At least he'd know what he was doing.

Boy, had he ever.

I spent a lot of time thinking about that night over the past year and a half. Lots of lonely nights, remembering the feel of his arms around me. Imagining I still was wrapped up inside them.

It was weird, but I hadn't felt like he was seducing me. Even when he was taking advantage of my naivete, I had somehow felt safe.

Cherished even.

Maybe even loved a little.

That sounded crazy in retrospect but there it was. It wasn't his fault I was the most gullible virgin alive. He hadn't made any promises to me that night.

Not with words anyway. With his eyes... his lips... his hands. Well, that was on me for interpreting things as if I lived in a fairy tale. I lived in the real world, and things just didn't happen that way.

And he'd given me Hallie. She'd changed everything of course. Put college plans on hold for the foreseeable future.

But she was perfect and I loved her more than I could have imagined. It was like she was covered in some sort of magical pixie dust that made me turn into goo. I loved her more than my own life, and that was the truth.

I laughed. It was a good thing too, considering how much poop she seemed to make. I wondered if it was all babies or just mine.

It seemed like a whole lot of poop.

"Hey Jenny. You got a table."

I nodded at Margery, grabbing my tray and pad. I still wrote everything down, though she said I wouldn't have to forever. I was still green but I was learning. It was a good thing too.

As an unwed mother without a degree of any sort, I had a feeling I'd be waiting tables for a long time. I didn't mind. It was honorable work, and Hallie was worth having sore feet.

I made a note to get some more practical shoes with my first paycheck as I headed towards the back, absentmindedly looking around. There was a table in the back that had been empty last time I looked. I saw the guy at the table and froze.

You have got to be fucking kidding me.

It was him. He was here. Jagger himself.

Speak of the ever lovin' devil.

My heart started to pound as I forced my feet to go forward. I couldn't run and hide, even if that was what I wanted to do. I also had an absurd urge to adjust my skirt. Fix my hair. Put on some lipstick.

But I didn't. I had a job to do and that was that. I stepped up to the table and tucked the tray under my arm, pulling out my pad and a pencil.

"Good evening. Can I take your order?"

He looked up at me and smiled. The slow, arrogant smile of a man who knows a woman intimately. Who knows what she looks like naked.

"Hello there, sugarlips."

I felt my palm twitch. I had a sudden desire to smack that knowing, sensual smile off his handsome face. And he was handsome. More than I remembered.

No wonder Hallie was so gorgeous, damn him. I hadn't realized until that moment the extent of the resemblance. With her dark hair and tawny skin, she was a version of him in miniature.

Our daughter looked just like him.

Especially the eyes.

"May I take your order?"

"What, no hello? It's been a while, sweetheart, but I never forgot you."

He leaned back in his seat, giving me a look up and down. He rubbed his lower lip, making an expression almost like he was in pain. He didn't even bother to hide it when he leisurely checked out my chest.

"Hmmfff... Oh yeah, I thought about you a lot."

I turned red, hoping it was too dark for him to see it.

"Can I take your order?"

He patted the seat next to him.

"Come and take a load off. "

34

"I can't. I'm working. And I wouldn't anyway."

"Why not, Jenny?"

He gave me a hurt look, his big blue eyes looking sad. Like a puppy who'd been deprived of a bone.

"You used to like me, remember?"

I looked around furtively, then leaned forward. I braced my hands on the table and hissed at him. I had just about had it with his bullshit, and he'd been here less than five freakin' minutes.

"I need this job. Tell me what you want so I can do it."

He held his hands up in surrender. Then he picked up the menu and perused it. But he kept stealing glances at my legs.

Not just my legs.

I could have sworn he was staring *between* them.

I grit my teeth and waited.

"Two shots. Tequila. One pitcher of beer. And one plate of ribs."

"Sides?"

He stared at my breasts and shook his head in awe.

"Hmmfff... I'll take the biscuits."

I wrote it down and tucked my pencil away. Then I cleared some empty beers off his table.

"Margery will bring your drinks."

He caught my arm, stopping me from leaving. He really was a caveman. Acting like he thought I was going to sleep with him again! After everything I found out about him? Even if he was oozing sex in every direction.

Hell no.

"Why not you?"

I smiled at him sweetly.

"I'm too young to serve the alcohol."

He blanched, his face so pale I thought I saw a smattering of freckles. I turned around, walking away with a definite spring in my step.

Score: Jenny - One. Jagger - Zero.

3

JAGGER

I licked the sauce off my fingers, watching Jenny work. Feldon had been right. This place *did* have the best barbeque south of the Mississippi.

But the amazing ribs were not half as good as the view.

Sweet Jesus, Jenny was finer than what I'd conjured up in my imagination. Her legs were just as long as I remembered but the rest of her was... different. She'd filled out even more, keeping that hourglass shape that drove me nuts last time we'd met. And then some.

She was a brick house.

And I would love to have a visit inside. Hell, not a visit. I wanted to take up permanent residence.

Too bad she wasn't as happy to see me as I was to see her.

I frowned, rubbing my face. I had to wonder why that was. Maybe she'd asked around about me... Yeah, that would do it.

I had quite a reputation amongst the Marines.

But I was a reformed man now. Or I would be, if she gave me another shot. I tilted my head, wondering why she was here. Again. Off another base.

My eyes got wide. I must be an idiot. She was either a military groupie or had a family member in the service. Just... which one? Husband? No. She wasn't wearing a ring and she didn't strike me as the cheating type. Parent? She wasn't *that* young.

It wasn't falling into place for me. Sweet little Jenny was a mystery. I would figure it out though. And I would make her mine. Or at least soften her up enough to take another crack at it.

If she was a groupie, I didn't care. There were women who had a thing for soldiers, officers in particular. I'd convert her to a one man woman. Just like she'd done to me, the first time I saw those emerald eyes of hers. Hell, if she let me, I'd stick to her like glue.

If she was... related to someone... or an Army brat... well, I might be in bigger trouble than I realized.

I might have to contend with a big brother or a daddy, whoever the unlucky bastard was. I tried to imagine having a daughter that looked like Jenny. It would be hell. Especially since she did not seem to know her effect on men.

And she was innocent enough to work in a place like this and think she wouldn't be dealing with a hard dick or twelve every damn minute. I started getting upset just thinking about it. This was no place for a sweet girl like her. It wasn't safe.

I was going to have to protect her. I'd see her home each night, starting tonight. Hopefully, back to my place.

To my bed.

And that's all there was to it.

I watched as she 'accidentally' spilled a glass of water on a customer. I grinned. He must've said something cheeky to her. So, maybe she could take care of herself.

Didn't mean she didn't need backup.

And I was just the man for the job.

She went behind the bar and picked up a huge box of empties. I was across the room in a flash. I was grinning as I tried to take the box from her.

"I got this sweetheart."

"Let go!"

"What? Why? No need to trouble your pretty little arms."

"My *what?*"

Oh boy. Her eyes were green fire as she wrenched the box out of my hands and flounced into the back. I followed her, a little less confident than I'd been a few minutes ago.

"What's wrong, sweetheart? What got you so riled up?"

She spun around and hissed at me. Like a pissed off kitty cat. I leaned against the door and grinned. I liked kitties. Especially gorgeous ones like her.

"I need this job, Jagger! Don't ruin it for me like you-"

I straightened up. This was not regular grade anger. This was a bonafide grudge.

"Like I what?"

She scowled at me mutinously.

"Nothing."

I smiled again.

"Well, if it reall is nothing, when are you going to let me take you out again?"

"How about never?"

"Oh come on sweetheart, we had a good time together, didn't we?"

She looked like she was about to cough. Or choke. Her eyes were wide, practically bulging, as she seemed to struggle for air. I was about to get her a glass of water when she burst out laughing.

And kept laughing.

She laughed so hard she had to bend forward and rest her hands on her knees.

I stopped smiling.

"What's so damn funny?"

"You are Jagger. I'm surprised you even remember me with all your floozies."

"I don't have any floozies."

I glanced at the heavens, expecting lightning to strike.

"Well, not anymore."

She just looked at me. I could see I'd hurt her somehow. I didn't like that.

Not one bit.

"Come on sweetheart, let's talk."

"I can't. And don't call me that."

I raised an eyebrow at her.

"You can't talk? You're doing just fine."

"No, I mean not here. I'm not supposed to... fraternize."

"Says who?"

She sighed.

"My boss, that's who."

JENNY

I sighed, staring at the gorgeous, stubborn, sexy as hell man giving me his best puppy dog eyes.

"Fine, Jagger. I can take my break now I guess. We can talk out back."

I was being soft. I knew it. But Jagger had looked so crestfallen. And I knew he wouldn't give up.

Besides, I was sort of exaggerating the fraternizing part. No one had mentioned that. But I didn't want to get in trouble. I'd just started the damn job and I needed it.

The owner, Gary, had been reluctant to hire me to begin with. I wasn't even twenty-one. But the night manager Margery had persuaded him that I would be good for business. She may have used the phrase 'eye candy.'

I just couldn't drink in the place.

Which was fine. I couldn't drink anyway. If I did I would have to pump and dump.

No way Hallie was getting boozy breast milk!

I leaned out and signaled to Margery. She nodded and I glanced at Jagger. He was watching me with a dark intensity that gave me chills.

All the way to my lady parts.

"Okay, let's go."

"After you, sweetheart."

Jagger followed me through the stock room to the door that we got deliveries through. It was also the garbage loading area. So it stank.

Even though we hosed it down twice a day.

I walked out and kept going. In the far back was a picnic table for the staff to take lunch if the weather was nice. It was out of sight behind a freestanding concrete wall.

Apparently, lots of people screwed back here.

But I didn't really want to talk about that.

I turned and crossed my arms.

"Go ahead. Talk."

He started to sit on the picnic table.

"I wouldn't do that. Not until it's been hosed down."

"Why?"

"I heard it gets more use than a motel mattress."

He grinned at me.

"It's still early. I doubt anyone has used it tonight."

I shrugged. He had a point. I noticed he still didn't take a seat. He just looked at me, really taking me in. I looked away. It's not that he made me uncomfortable exactly. But he was so intense. I wasn't used to that sort of scrutiny.

Well, except on my ass.

"You aren't like I remember you."

I tossed my hair. He was getting to me already and he knew it. I was being pulled in by his gravitational force. And I hated him for it.

"Easy? Gullible? Stupid?"

He shook his head, his eyes studying me.

"No, you seemed determined to be bad that night. I was more than happy to help."

I sighed. I might as well tell him. For some reason I found myself telling him the truth.

"I was going through a phase. After my mother died, I spent a lot of time rebelling. I drank and snuck out at night. I even dyed my hair purple."

"Purple?"

"Yep. A few months before you met me. It... wasn't a very long phase. Not that it matters."

He looked at me, listening. He was more present than anyone I'd ever talked to before. Maybe that was his appeal.

Or his dimples.

Or his broad shoulders and thick arms.

Or his ass.

I looked away, trying to ignore the rush of desire I felt. The attraction was still there. Unfortunately.

"I'm sorry. I lost my family too."

I swallowed, feeling something all too familiar well up behind my eyes. Tears. Jagger was going to make me cry.

Damn him. He wasn't playing fair. He wasn't supposed to have his own sad story.

He wasn't supposed to be nice.

But my mother had raised me to use good manners. So I wasn't going to be rude. Besides, I had a sudden feeling he was telling the truth.

"I'm sorry, too."

He looked at the ground, then at the sky, then back at me.

"So, you are out of your wild phase?"

I nodded. He grinned and reached for me. "Me too."

I gasped as he pulled me against him. His body felt good. The heat of him felt good.

He felt good.

"But I'd love to get wild with you."

His lips came crashing down on mine. I made a sound that was half protest, half surrender. I was frozen as his lips angled over mine, encouraging them to open.

With a moan, I gave in and opened my lips. Instantly, the kiss went wild. We were all over each other, practically inhaling each other as our tongues tangled. It was not a gentle kiss. It was not a sweet kiss.

It was a Jagger kiss.

Then I felt his hands close over my ass cheeks and squeeze. I remembered what he really wanted. What he was after. One thing and one thing only. I remembered the manwhore he was.

I remembered how he'd knocked me up.

I loved my baby girl with all my heart, but I did not need to be a single mother with TWO mini-Jaggers running amuck.

I reared back and slapped him with everything I had. His head swung to the side and then back. He stared at me, clearly shocked. He probably didn't believe that there was a woman on Earth that could resist him.

I lifted my finger, pointing it in his face.

"Don't you ever, *ever* kiss me again!"

I pushed away from him and stalked to the back door of the bar. My heart was racing. My lips were tingling. My hand stung from smacking his surprisingly smooth and soft skinned face. Halfway across the parking lot I turned and shouted.

"And don't call me sweetheart!"

4
JAGGER

I rubbed my cheek where she'd slapped it, admiring the way she looked in those tight jeans of hers as she stomped off. She was a redhead alright. Only a russet haired woman would slap a man after kissing the hell out of him.

And Jenny was one hell of a kisser.

I took my time coming back in. Not because I was worried she'd slap me again. I was just deep in thought.

Mostly thinking about gettin' deep in her.

I sat down and ordered a watered down pitcher of beer. I had a long night ahead of me. I had someone to walk home.

Jenny scowled at me while she took my order, and scowled when she watched the other bartender bring it back. She scowled when she brought me a basket of fries.

The woman basically scowled up and down the whole night.

I sat back and waited for her shift to end, enjoying the memory of the way her luscious body had melted against me. It was getting close to time when she asked me if I wanted anything else. I took my time, staring up and down her body.

"Oh yeah honey, I can think of a lot of things."

"I'm not a piece of meat, Jagger!"

"No, you're definitely not a piece of meat. But you do look tender."

Jenny threw my check at me and turned tail to see to her other tables. I made my last beer count, sipping it slow as molasses until I was the last guy in the place. She started getting ready to close up. She 'accidentally' mopped right over my boots.

I smiled and stood up, throwing a fifty-dollar tip on the table. Her eyes widened. She stared at me as I walked out of the bar.

'Course I was waiting out front for her when she came out fifteen minutes later.

She stared at me. I stared at her. Then she walked up to me and tossed that fifty-dollar bill in my face.

"I'm not for sale you sonofabitch!"

I looked right at her. She was angry. But she had mistaken my meaning.

"I didn't say you were."

"Then what are you doing tipping like that?"

"I took up a seat in your section all night. Seemed fair."

She stared at me belligerently.

"Well, I'm not taking it."

"How about a twenty?"

"What are you, a cash machine?"

She huffed, crossing her arms over her chest. Her glorious, perfect, mind-bending chest. I pulled out a ten and a five.

"Fifteen?"

She yanked the money out of my hand so fast I got rug burn. Then she stomped off. The woman had a pair of legs on her. And she made good use of them.

I was whistling as I followed her back towards the base.

JENNY

I was enjoying the memory of Jagger's face after I'd slapped it when I stopped in the middle of the road. Someone was behind me. I knew who it was before I even turned around.

Yep, Jagger was trailing me. I shooed him away. He just smiled at me, like the daft man that he was. I stomped my foot in frustration, kicking up dust on the gravel road.

"Are you a stray dog?"

"No."

"Then stop following me!"

"I'm not following you. I'm escorting you."

"Ha!"

I kept walking. He kept following. I stopped again, pointing my finger at him.

"You are either the dumbest or the bravest man alive."

He grinned.

"Shoot, honey. Why can't I be both?"

I scowled at him, suspicion dawning. I pointed at him again, wagging my finger.

"You just want to know where I live!"

He shrugged.

"I sure would like to sweetheart but that's not what this is about."

"Then what?"

"Look around, cupcake. There is no one around for miles. It's not a safe walk to take alone at one in the morning."

"Oh, so you are going to protect me?"

He nodded smugly.

"That's right, buttercup."

"I'm not a fucking buttercup. Or your honey. Or a cupcake!"

He whistled.

"You sure have a mouth on you. I'd like to sweeten that up for you."

I made a sound of pure aggravation and turned to continue walking. He was right though. I wasn't super psyched to be out here all by myself. I wished I had my old ten-speed. Maybe it was still in the garage...

I rode it all over the last base we lived on. Before I got knocked up by you-know-who. That reminded me that he was still behind me. If he followed me the whole way home, he might accidentally meet my dad or worse yet, get a good look at Hallie.

I had to distract him. Shake him somehow. He could not find out where I lived on the base.

I waited until we were just inside the base and stopped. I looked over my shoulder and gave him a come-hither look. It wasn't all that hard to pretend I wanted him to kiss me.

Especially since part of me *did* want him to kiss me.

The sad, pathetic, lonely part.

The part that was susceptible to wavy haired hunks who followed them home.

And hormones. I had a lot of hormones. And pretty much all of them were in favor of making out with Jagger.

He raised an eyebrow as I crooked my finger, sauntering off towards one of the less populated areas of the base. I leaned against the side of an empty house and waited. I figured he might assume I lived near here when I took off in a couple of minutes.

After I'd scratched the itch.

Jagger was right behind me, almost touching me when I turned. Well, he certainly didn't waste time. I guess you had to give him credit for that.

He stared at me hungrily as I tilted my head, looking at him.

"What changed your mind sweetheart?"

I grit my teeth at the endearment, forcing a sickly sweet smile.

"You did, Jagger. You're a true gentleman, did you know that?"

He looked like he was blushing as he stepped closer. He was inches away. Suddenly I felt breathless and lightheaded. then I peered at him in the darkness.

He *was* blushing!

Derek Jagger, blushing. Who would have thought it?

I reached out and grabbed one of his belt loops, tugging him against me. His eyes flared, locked onto my lips. I licked mine and he moaned.

Whatever else he was, he was not faking his attraction to me. Even if he was a manwhore, this was real. His reputation was for loving them and leaving them, not following girls home and blushing when they pulled him into an alleyway.

I felt strange suddenly.

Guilty almost.

I revised my earlier plan to tase or pepper spray him. I was always protected, and carried a taser and hot spray. I had since I was 13 years old. Daddy dearest had seen to that.

No, Jagger did not deserve the taser.

I would just trick him instead.

There. My conscience was clear. I would kiss him and then run off on him. That seemed fair, all things considered.

That's the last thing I thought for a while, because Jagger was kissing me. I couldn't help the soft moan of pleasure as he pressed himself against me. His hands were all over me, sneaking around my waist and hips, tugging me hard against his chest.

Our lips and tongues seemed to know exactly what to do and when. How hard and how fast... or slow. We were in perfect synchronicity as our heads twisted and turned, trying to get deeper... closer... more intimate.

Speaking of intimacy...

Jagger was hard. Really hard and really big. I'd remembered the size of him just fine, despite the heavy drinking we'd done that night. But maybe I had blocked out the size of his unit.

I'd remembered big. Huge even.

This was... bigger.

I whimpered as he started to push his hips against me. He lifted my thigh and lowered himself slightly so he could grind into me from below. My head fell back and he started kissing my neck.

I wanted more. I wanted a bed. I wanted him inside me.

No, Jenny! Bad! No, no, no!

I pushed against his shoulder breathlessly. If we didn't stop, he was going to fuck me right out here. Up against this house. Or on the ground. Outside, where anyone could see us.

Hell, I had a feeling I might be the one fucking *him*.

For some reason, I was just easy when Jagger was involved. All the more reason for me to stay away from him. Permanently.

"Jagger- ohhh... hmmfff... I, um, I... I have to pee!"

He lifted his head from my throat. I had the distinct impression he'd been aiming for my boobs. If he'd started doing his crazy tongue work on my bare flesh, I would not have been able to stop.

So, in the nick of time, basically.

"Now?"

"Yes. Sorry. Now. I'll just pee over there."

"We could go back to my place instead..."

"Can't. No time. It's an emergency."

He cursed and ran his hand through his hair. Then he stepped back. I smiled at him and he grabbed me, kissing me hard.

"Hurry back, sweet Jenny."

I nodded, practically stumbling away. I hurried through the buildings, zigzagging my way to the other side of the base where my father's house was. I felt oddly guilty as I ran away from him.

My dad was watching TV and didn't notice my dishelleved appearance as I walked through the living room to shower. I closed my eyes as the hot water ran over my body. But nothing could take away the feeling of his hands on me.

I could still see the look on Jagger's face as I promised him I'd be right back as I snuck into Hallie's room and gave her a soft kiss.

5
JAGGER

I stood there, not believing this was happening. One minute Jenny was putty in my hands and then poof. She'd run off on me.

Again.

It had taken me almost ten minutes to realize it. I'd been waiting patiently, pleasantly contemplating the night ahead. Then I'd started to get suspicious of her motives.

She'd been awfully angry. Then she'd been awfully agreeable. Then she was... gone.

Sweet, sexy, *conniving* Jenny was gone.

She'd tricked me, plain and simple. I ran after her, not just to yank her into my arms. I also wanted to ask her why. I was riled up but good. She'd played the classic bait and switch on me. But why bother? She could have told me to go to hell just as easy.

Unless... she just didn't want me to know where she lived.

Maybe she had a man. Maybe she'd moved on. It wasn't a stretch by any means. It had been a long while since our night together after all, and she was a damn fine woman. I was sure dozens of men had tried to tie her down since I saw her last.

Hell, probably hundreds.

But if she had a man, why would she kiss me like that? She wanted me, whether she knew it or not. And Jenny didn't strike me as a tease. She'd been a damn virgin the last time I saw her!

Maybe she was making up for lost time now that I'd deflowered her. But if that was true... she would have taken me up on my offer to go back to my place. I knew I'd pleased her the last time we were together. And then some.

I was jogging through the base, just on the off chance I might catch sight of her. But the whole time my mind was racing like an engine on overdrive. I would get to the bottom of this, come hell or high water.

Jenny was going to pay the piper, even if it was just an explanation.

I hoped it was a whole lot more than that though.

I went home after an hour of aimless wandering. I took a cold shower, trying to lose the wood she'd given me when we were fooling around. Two kisses. Two boners. All in one night.

I put a sheet on the bed and lay there, staring at the ceiling. It was unnerving how quiet the nights were after Iraq. No feral dogs barking. No bombs. No patrols.

Just... silence.

And tomorrow, I started my new job as an Instructor Pilot. There were manuals to study and new Marines to train. I knew I was going to be a good teacher. I knew the aircraft they'd be learning on inside and out.

I just didn't know if I was going to like being stuck in one place. Not without something sweet and pretty to come home to each night. If I had a girl though... if I had Jenny...

Well hell, I'd be the luckiest guy on the base.

Hell, I'd be the luckiest guy on the damn planet.

I closed my eyes and smiled. Jenny had done the impossible it seemed. She was domesticating me, without even trying.

I just hoped she'd let me domesticate her back.

JENNY

"More eggs, Dad?"

He nodded, wiping his lips.

"You're a fine cook 'Niffer. Your mother would be proud."

I scrambled the eggs, adding the low sodium seasoning the doctor's recommended for dad. I didn't look up. I didn't want him to see the tears in my eyes.

I was way too emotional this morning. I must have been hormonal or something. It had nothing at all to do with Jagger's unexpected return, or how he'd looked at me... or how he'd kissed me...

Or how I'd felt after I left him high and dry thinking he had a willing woman on his hands...

Definitely not that.

I did not feel even remotely guilty about that. Why should I? He was a player. So what if he liked me? He liked all women. Maybe I was just one in a hundred.

Actually, from what I'd heard that's exactly what I was.

But more like one in a thousand.

Still, even if he was promiscuous, he wasn't entirely unlikable. It had been considerate of him to walk me home last night, even if he had ulterior motives. And that tip he'd tried to give me... well, he was extragantly generous.

He had some very nice qualities, and I wasn't just talking about his looks.

Hopefully Hallie would inherit some of those as well. It was too bad he wasn't real daddy material. I sighed, It would be awfully nice to have his help raising our little girl.

I knew I'd have to tell him about his daughter at some point. That would be the end of his pursuit of me though. And for some reason, I wasn't ready to do that.

It was so... final.

Once he found out how fertile I was, how tied down he would be, I knew he'd run for the damn hills.

I turned the heat off and served dad a few more eggs. I had more important things to worry about than Jagger and his wandering dick.

Hallie cooed from her high chair and I kissed her head.

"You working again tonight?"

I nodded.

"Thanks for looking after her. I'll be able to afford a sitter soon."

He waved his hand, brushing me off. He took a bite of his breakfast and looked at me. Then he set his fork down again.

"Jenny..."

Uh oh, I could sense another one of his famous talks coming. My dad was used to being in charge of soldiers. He was prone to giving speeches that involved words like 'discipline' and 'rules.'

"You know I don't approve of what you did. Having unprotected... relations with some stranger. It was selfish and risky and irresponsible."

I grit my teeth, swallowing my retort.

"But I'm proud of you for how you've handled everything that came after. You gave up a lot for your little girl. And... you're a good mother."

My jaw must have dropped because he flushed. My dad never said nice things like that. Praise was rare in our house and always had been. That was two compliments in a row, and it wasn't even eight o'clock in the morning.

I poured him another cup of half decaf/ half caff and sat down to feed Hallie. She'd already had a few spoonfulls and I liked to feed her slow. It kept her spit ups to a minimum.

I fed her and myself, alternating bites. She cooed at me, shaking her hands in excitement. I wondered why she was in such a good mood today. She seemed even happier than usual, and that was saying something.

Personally, I was feeling the opposite of happy. I was depressed and worried about Jagger. How I would avoid him... How I would deal with the Hallie situation...

How I would resist him...

I cleaned up the kitchen, wiping down the counter with a baby wipe. I used a fresh wipe on Hallie's cheeks and then used it on my own face. No time to shower. We had to get out and get some fresh air before it got too hot.

Morning was prime playground time. I'd even made friends with some of the other moms. Well, one of them anyway. A few of them seemed to take an issue with the fact that Hallie didn't have a daddy on the base.

I sighed.

If only they knew.

I got her dressed and pulled on jeans and a clean-ish t-shirt. I pulled my hair into a high ponytail, tucked it into a baseball cap and glanced in the mirror. I swiped on some lipgloss and was out the door not soon after my dad.

I pushed her stroller through the base, feeling like I was on a mission.

Operation Avoid Jagger

I slid on my oversized sunglasses. They had belonged to my mother, one of the things of hers I'd managed to hang onto. A few impossibly soft t-shirts, some plain gold jewelry, and her sunnies. She had a big collection of them and I put them all into rotation.

These were the biggest though, and therefore the best disguise.

And I needed the disguise. I was desperate to avoid you-know-who. At least with Hallie in tow. I knew I'd see him at the bar again soon. Maybe even tonight.

There was no way I was going to avoid him forever.

I wasn't even sure I wanted to...

I waved to my friend Crystal as I pushed Hallie's stroller into the playground. I sat and pulled out a bottle of water, watching Hallie play in the sand box. The sprinkler was on too, but she was way too small to go in with the bigger kids running around in there.

Maybe in a year I'd let her play in there. That's if I was still here. And that was a big 'if.' The minute I made enough money at the bar I would hightail it out of here so fast that heads would spin.

I sighed. It would be hard to leave dad, but I had my own life to build. And this was not the best place to start it... it was hard to meet guys when you were an unwed mother who also happened to be the daughter of the highest ranking officer on base.

Not that I needed a man, but... it would be nice to go on a date once in a while. And college. The nearest school was an hour away. And I would need money to pay a sitter all day while I sat in classes.

Soon Jenny. When Hallie was a little older, I'd do it. I'd get that education my mother had always wanted for me.

"Earth to Jenny! Where is your head today?"

I grimaced, smiling apologetically at Crystal. She was a smart ass, and cool as fuck. She was pretty much my best friend in the whole world.

And a lot less high in the instep about hanging out with a single unwed mother than the rest of the young moms.

She handed me a stick of gum and I took it, popping it into my mouth.

"Thanks Crys. I... um... bumped into someone last night."

She pulled down her aviator glasses and gave me a look.

"Who?"

"No one. He just *used* to be someone."

"Uh huh."

She gave me the look again and shook her head. Her chin length hair was artificially colored a bright cool auburn. It was also straightened and styled to the max. She might not be a natural redhead, but she had enough sass to pull it off.

Not to mention inch long fire engine red fingernails and perfectly applied makeup.

We called ourselves 'The Reds.'

It was just another thing that made us different from the rest of the moms. Though

Crystal was happily married to a Marine, like most of the other playground moms. I was... not.

"You will tell me everything."

I snuck a glance at her. I probably *would* tell her everything. But not yet. I was still figuring out how the hell I felt about Jagger showing up like this.

That's when I saw him. He was walking and talking with a group of young Marines. Fresh recruits from the look of it. They fell in step behind him.

He turned his head and I could have sworn he saw me.

Right before I hit the ground and rolled under the bench we were sitting on. Crystal was laughing uproariously as I peeked out. The marching soldiers had moved on, so I could only see the back of Jagger's head.

I tried not to stare at his cute little butt.

I didn't think he'd seen me, thank the good lord.

"Don't tell me-"

She was laughing to bust a gut as I brushed myself off and sat back down next to her.

"That was 'someone'?"

I shrugged sheepishly and nodded. She fluffed her hair dramatically and smacked her lips.

"He's fine girl. What's the hold up?"

"He's a manwhore. *That's* the hold up."

"Oh, whatever. Everyone is a tramp before they settle down."

She looked at the trio of uptight moms giving us dirty looks from across the playground.

"Well, everyone interesting anyway."

She turned towards me, clearly wanting the full scoop.

"Who is he anyway?"

"His name's Jagger. He's... I guess he's kind of nice. When he's not trying to dick every woman in sight."

"And now he wants to dick you?"

I nodded.

"Yeah. He has no idea I'm a mom though."

"So what?"

"I... I just want to avoid him for now okay?"

She smiled.

"Sure, but that's not going to stop my mission to get you laid. You don't have to fall in love or get married, even though I think you should. Just get something up in there."

I laughed, shaking my head.

"I'm serious girl. If you don't use it, it might dry up and fly away on you. And then you wouldn't have a pussy."

I was cackling at Crystal's dirty mouth when the strong hands appeared on the bench behind me. I froze, knowing who it was before he said a word. Only one person on base would invade my personal space that way.

Well, other than Jagger.

Lieutenant Davis.

"Hey Crystal. Hey Jenny."

His eyes were all over me as he came around to stand by the side of the bench. Davis was the latest in the single soldiers that Crystal kept trying to 'accidentally' introduce me too. I refused set-ups but she was relentless.

So was Clyde Davis.

He was good looking, with dark hair and piercing eyes. He was tall and built and always polite. And he knew about Hallie.

For some reason, I wasn't sure yet if I wanted to go out with him. I was starting to lean towards a definite 'no.' Something about him made me feel a little bit... slimy.

"Uh, hi."

I hoped he hadn't heard what we were talking about before he showed up. I needn't have worried though. The man was slightly obsessed with himself.

"How's the new job going?"

I glanced at Crystal. Her husband had served with Clyde. That's how she knew him. She must have told him I got a job at the juke joint.

"Good. How are you?"

He sat down beside me and launched into a monologue about how he'd impressed his CO again. I stared at his shoes, noticing the perfect polish on them. I had a sudden vision of his closet, all neatly pressed uniforms and perfectly shined shoes.

He never had a hair out of place either.

Not like Jagger's adorably tousled waves.

I bit my lip, wondering why I was comparing them. It's not like I was interested in Jagger anyway. Davis was a much better candidate.

Even if he bored me to tears.

6
JAGGER

I sipped coffee as I gave my lecture. This was a hell of a lot better than active duty. Nobody was bringing me a fresh cup of joe back then. I stared out at the newest crop of pilots. Their wide-open faces stared back at me, hanging on every word.

The kids were so wet behind the ears it made me feel like an old man.

Well, not old. Mature. Wise. And feeling oddly like it might be time to settle down.

I'd sworn up and down it would never happen to me. But then I'd met that gorgeous redhead. The girl kept me on my toes and kept me guessing. It wouldn't be boring to be stuck with her.

Not even a little.

Hell, I'd go to sleep every night with a smile on my face if she was curled up against me.

I grinned, remembering how she'd tried to duck and cover from me that morning. She had no idea how noticeable she was with that hair of hers. Even tucked under a cap I'd seen her from fifty paces.

I rubbed my chin thoughtfully.

So, my sweet Jenny was a babysitter and a bartender. Industrious little thing. At least I knew she lived on base for sure now. Maybe as a nanny.

That meant she liked kids. That was good. Because I'd like to make some with her.

A whole passel of them.

I clicked through the slides, carefully describing what I considered to be the most important parts of the practice jets they'd be training on. The twitchy fuel gauge. The almost overly responsive engines. The importance of never skipping a single step.

The dangers of getting cocky.

Of course, I was the cockiest pilot in the service, known for skipping protocol all the time. But there was no need to tell them that. I wanted them to do as I said, not as I did.

I sent them off to the mess hall for lunch and got up to stretch my legs. I walked back towards the playground, hoping to get another glimpse of my girl. I got there just in time to see her and her friend walking towards the market.

Perfect. I needed some groceries. And I could say hello to Jenny in the meantime.

Hell, that was a lie. I wanted to find out why she'd run out on me the night before. I wanted answers dammit.

I watched my quarry as they strolled along, having no idea they were being tracked. I was going to divide and conquer. Then I would interrogate the subject.

I'd get to the bottom of this before lunch was out. Then I'd ask her out on a proper date. Get some quality alone time with her.

I grinned and followed her into the grocery store. She headed straight for the produce aisle. I watched as she leaned forward, talking to the kid she was watching. Her face lit up with obvious affection for the baby.

God damn, the woman was fucking beautiful!

I'd give just about anything to have her look that way at me. I grabbed a basket and started putting things into it willy nilly, hurrying over until I could 'accidentally' bump into her cart.

She stood up sharply. I could tell she was about to give me a rude comment before she saw who it was. Those gorgeous eyes of hers got wide as saucers. I smiled at her, leaning against the melon display.

"Hi."

She just stared at me. Her friend on the other hand, was grinning ear to ear. She nudged Jenny out of the way, holding out her hand.

"I'm Crystal. And you are?"

I flashed a smile at her.

"Jagger."

She gave Jenny a look and cleared her throat.

"I think I'm going to get some ice cream. You want any, Jenny?"

She stared at me, ignoring her friend. I answered for her.

"Yes. She'll take... a big ole tub of Neapolitan. My treat."

Jenny's cheeks got red as her friend rolled away with a shit-eating grin on her face. Clearly the girls had talked about me. That was a good sign.

I hoped so anyway.

"What are you doing, Jagger?"

"Grocery shopping. A man needs to eat, doesn't he?"

She glanced at my basket and laughed.

"You must really like... bananas."

I looked at my cart. I had grabbed a lot of bananas. I coughed a little.

"They have a lot of potassium. Here, you should take some."

I tried to put some of my bananas into her basket. She gave me a look, then started rolling her cart away.

"I can shop for myself, Jagger."

"I know. You can do a lot of things. Like run out on a man. Why'd you do that anyway, Jenny?"

She stopped and looked at me. She chewed on her lower lip and I got all hot and bothered. I would love to be the one to do that for her.

"I'm sorry. It just... didn't seem like a good idea."

"What exactly didn't seem like a good idea?"

She sighed as if I was the most exasperating human on Earth. Hell, maybe I was. Didn't mean I wasn't going to win this argument.

"You know."

I stepped closer, lowering my voice to an intimate level.

"You mean kissing? Making out? Touching each other?"

Her mouth opened and her eyes lowered to my lips. I was inches from kissing her in the middle of the damn grocery store! But I didn't care. I was under her spell, just like she was under mine.

Then the baby she was looking after let out a soft squeal, breaking the spell. I looked down and smiled at the little cutie. She had soft round cheeks and adorable dimples.

"Aren't you a cutie?"

Jenny made an odd sound, like she was swallowing a curse. I gave her a look and bent down to the adorable baby. A chubby little hand reached out and patted my face.

"And what's your name, sweetheart?"

JENNY

This could not be happening.

THIS COULD NOT BE HAPPENING.

I stared as the arrogant, muscle bound, too-handsome-for-his-own-good fixed-wing fighter pilot leaned down over my baby. *Our baby.* And she cooed up at him, seeming to adore him on sight.

Jagger was meeting his daughter in the middle of the damned produce aisle!

Breathe Jenny. In and out. Easy does it. He doesn't know. She doesn't know. Nobody knows the truth but you.

I felt the world start to tilt.

"Hey, you okay?"

He was looking at me with concern. I nodded curtly, hoping he would change the damn subject. Move on. Hit on someone else.

"Wow, Jenny that is one cute kid. Makes me wish I had one of my own."

Jagger was smiling at me warmly. Did he mean... He licked his lips.

"Course, I need a woman for that."

My jaw dropped. Was he implying that he wanted a woman, just to... to breed?

"Maybe even a wife."

My jaw dropped a little farther. I didn't know what his game was, but I felt like I was being bamboozled. At the same time, his strategy was working.

I'd felt a leap of hope inside me. Jagger and me. For real. Together.

It sounded kind of awesome.

I mentally shook myself. I needed a slap in the face. I knew the reality. It was all an act. He was a player. Everyone said it. I knew it. I would not be fooled.

I grabbed a grapefruit without looking and put it in my cart. And then another. And then another.

"You know you can't just pick out a wife like you're picking out a- a-"

He smiled at me, his gorgeous eyes crinkling.

"A grapefruit?"

"Yes! Women are not fruit, just waiting around to be plucked by- by you! They have their own plans, and dreams, and ideas!"

He had a tender look on his face. Like he was seeing me. *Really* seeing me.

"I know that. You are a whole lot of woman, Jenny. I do wish I knew your last name though."

I stopped loading the cart with grapefruit and stared at him.

"What? Why?"

"So I know what it is before I ask you to change it."

My jaw was open again. He was basically saying he wanted to marry me. That was what he was saying right?

That was insane. He barely knew me. And he had no way of knowing about... what had happened while he was gone.

Who had happened.

Again, it was an act. Most women probably fell into his bed. Hell, they probably crawled up to the foot of it begging. So this was his... sneaky attempt at getting the one woman on Earth who wasn't falling for him and his bedroom eyes!

"You must really think highly of yourself, don't you?"

He shrugged.

"I think pretty highly of you. I'll show you how much. If you let me."

He reached out and took my hand.

"I don't think you need anymore grapefruit, Red."

I looked at my hand and then at my cart. I had about twenty grapefruit in there. I didn't even really like grapefruit. I just got them for my dad's cholesterol.

I coughed and put a few back. Jagger helped me. I wanted to swat his hand away.

"Can I walk you home? I have about twenty minutes before class starts again."

I shook my head, knowing my voice would be thick with emotion. I didn't want him to know what he was doing to me. Basically twisting me around and turning me inside out.

"Come on sweetheart. Can't we at least be friends?"

He held out his hand and I stared at it. Then I heard Crystal clearing her throat from behind me. I took his hand, looking at him as if he were an alien from another planet.

"Okay Jagger. We can be friends. But that's it."

He smiled and lifted my hand to kiss it. I shivered at the feel of those impossibly soft lips on my skin. He noticed too.

I hoped he didn't notice how hard my nipples were.

His smile was smug as he lowered my hand and gently let go of it.

I crossed my arms over my chest and his grin widened. Oh yes, he'd noticed. Arghhh!

"That's alright, sweet Jenny. I'm willing to wait."

I scowled at him and turned away. But not before he nodded at Crystal and winked at me.

"See you later."

7
JAGGER

Twenty-two hundred hours. That's what time I showed up. That gave me three hours to wait. Wait, eat ribs, and watch Jenny work.

And watching her work was a thing of beauty. She was poetry in motion. Hell on wheels. Sex on rollerskates.

I grinned and bit into another sweet barbeque rib. Hmm.. they were good. Not as good as what I had in mind for dessert though.

I'd wanted to come earlier but I thought that might make me look pathetic. I didn't want Jenny to think I was desperate. Besides, I needed to get my house in order.

In case I had company later.

Female company.

Red headed company.

Jenny company.

She walked past, carrying a tray of empty beer bottles. I leaned my chin on my fist and made eyes at her. She gave me a suspicious look but stopped and put her tray down.

"Do you need something, Jagger?"

"Yes."

She pulled out her pad and waited expectantly.

"You want to try the cheesecake?"

"I want you."

"Jagger..."

I changed my tactics. As tempting as it was to try and get her into bed tonight, that didn't seem to be flying. I wanted to do this right anyway.

"I want to take you on a date."

She raised an eyebrow.

"I don't have time to go on a date-"

"I'm not finished. I want to take you out someplace special. Get you real dolled up and drink champagne. Then afterwards, I want to take you home and do things that would make a gynecologist blush."

Her mouth opened.

"I want to lick you. Every inch. And then I want to lick you again. You tasted so good, Jenny. I never forgot the way you tasted. Or looked. Or felt."

I smiled at her, knowing I had her under my spell. She blinked and her lips opened. I was hoping to see a little bit of drool.

"I wonder if you taste as good as I remember. I can't wait to find out."

She just stared at me, a dazed look on her face. I saw her throat move as she gulped. I sat back and took a long swig of my beer. But the whole time, I was looking at her.

And her lady parts.

She had such nice lady parts.

I set the beer down and leaned forward.

"And after I've had you six ways from Sunday- after you've had all you can take- I want to hold you in my arms all damn night. Every night Jenny. What do you think of that?"

Jenny was as still as a statue.

"Hell, I'll even make you breakfast."

She blinked at that. I smiled tenderly. The woman looked like no man had ever tried to seduce her before. It was adorable.

"Waitress!"

"Jenny, you got customers!"

Slowly, she reached down to pick up her tray. I watched as she walked across the room to the bar and set it down. She looked like she'd been hypnotized. I wasn't surprised.

I had that effect on women sometimes.

It was almost midnight when she came back with a small plate and set it down in front of me.

"What's this?"

"Cheesecake. It's on the house."

I grinned at her, feeling very pleased with the turn of events.

"You shouldn't have, darlin'."

"I didn't. Marge did. Said you were a good customer."

She shrugged self-consciously.

"She said you kept the fights to a minimum."

"I do?"

"You look sort of intimidating sitting over here by yourself you know."

I smiled at her sensuously.

"Oh."

She started to turn away and then stopped. When she looked back at me, there was a vulnerable look on her face. As if what she was about to say wasn't easy. I waited, utterly focused on her.

"Are you going to follow me home again tonight, Jagger?"

I nodded slowly.

"What about the night after that?"

I nodded again.

"Why?"

"Because I want to keep you safe. Because I can't get you out of my mind. I thought about you the whole time I was over there, Jenny."

"No lie?"

I shook my head.

"No lie, Red."

She closed her eyes, apparently coming to some sort of decision.

"Alright, Jagger. You win."

"I do?"

She nodded.

"I'll go out with you. And... you can walk me home if you want."

She shrugged slightly.

"You just might not like what you find."

I studied her.

"Try me, sweetheart. I can handle it."

She looked at me, her eyes dark with feeling.

"Just remember you said that."

JENNY

I stared straight ahead, wondering if I was crazy. I was weak. I knew that. I had given in, unable to continue resisting him. Jagger was more than charismatic and charming. *He was magnetic.*

And I was like a moth drawn to his flame.

I just hoped he was telling the truth. It sounded crazy after everything I'd learned about him when he was gone. But in my gut, somehow, I believed him.

And even if he was lying... well, at least I'd get to scratch the itch that I seemed to have for him and him alone. The fact of the matter was, Jagger made me horny.

Really, really horny.

He was walking beside me, close enough to take my hand. The back of his hand was warm as it brushed against mine. Once. Twice.

On the third time, his fingers snaked around mine, and squeezed.

And just like that, I was holding hands with Derek Jagger.

It was hard to describe the thrill that went through me at that simple gesture. It was so sweet and natural. I felt the ice around my heart start to melt. Just a little, but it melted all the same.

We walked like that until we got to the officer's housing. Jagger gave me a look and stopped. I looked at the incredulous look on his face with a soft smile.

"You live in here?"

I nodded and led the way towards the biggest house on the complex. I led him up the steps to the front porch. Now Jagger stopped and tugged my hand. His eyes were bright as he stared at me with an inquisitive look on his face.

"Wait- Jenny- are you a nanny for someone important?"

I shook my head.

"No."

"But-"

I stepped towards him and ran my fingertip down his chest.

"Do you want to talk? Or do you want to kiss me?"

He stared at me in the darkness.

"Kiss. Definitely kiss."

I slid both of my hands up his chest to his shoulders and smiled.

"Good."

He stared at my lips hungrily as he came closer... closer... with a moan he pulled me against him. I sighed as we came together. Our lips and tongues were seeking, stroking, twisting against each other. He held me by the waist, molding my body against his.

I'd said it before but it bore repeating.

Jagger was one hell of a kisser.

This was different than any kiss he'd given me before though. Tender. Caring. Possessive.

Devoted.

I was clutching his shoulders for dear life after just a few minutes. Then he froze. Jagger jumped back and I stared at him, wondering why he'd stopped so abruptly.

The front door of the house had opened.

"Niffer? Who's this?"

I opened my eyes and saw my father standing in the open doorway with a very, very unhappy look on his face.

Uh oh.

Jagger was about to meet the General.

Maybe I should have warned him after all.

8
JAGGER

I stared at General Reeds where he filled the doorway with his broad shoulders. He didn't just fill the space either. He ate it up. He *loomed*.

I did the only thing I could do.

I saluted.

Everyone knew General Reeds was the toughest motherfucker to set foot on American soil. Or Middle Eastern soil. Or anywhere there had been a conflict in the last thirty years or so.

The man was a fucking legend.

"'Niffer? Care to explain what you are doing with this young man?"

"Dad, this is Sergeant Derek Jagger. Jagger, this is... my dad."

I looked at her and back at the General. Then back again. I nodded to myself, as if something had just fallen into place.

Of course, she was the daughter of the guy who ran the entire damn show.

Naturally that was the particular pile of shit I would land in. He was looking at me like something he'd scraped off his damn boots. *After* he'd stomped on it.

This wasn't going to be easy.

But it was worth it.

She was worth it.

"At ease, Sergeant."

Now he was giving me a piercing stare. Like he was a farmer and I was the weasel in his henhouse. And he wasn't far off. I had been kissing the beejesus out of his daughter. Hell, I'd been ready to toss her over my shoulder and take her back to my lair, caveman style.

This was it. Time to man up. It was now or never, Jagger. I stood up straight, my eyes clear and my voice strong.

"Sir, I would like to call on you at a more convenient time and state my intentions toward your daughter."

He looked at me. Then he nodded.

"I hoped to take her to dinner tomorrow night."

"Tomorrow evening then. Be here at eighteen hundred hours. Then we'll see about you taking my daughter out. Come inside, Jennifer."

"Honestly, you two-"

"Come inside 'Niffer. Now."

Jenny gave me an exasperated look. She looked irritated by the exchange. I wanted to kiss her until she was melting against me again.

But I restrained myself for obvious reasons.

"Tomorrow night, Sergeant."

"Yes, sir."

"Don't be late."

"No, sir."

He pulled Jenny inside and shut the door in my face.

All the same I was whistling as I walked down the walkway to the sidewalk. I glanced back at the imposing house and shook my head.

After all this time, all this wondering, all this waiting, I finally had her last name. I had her number now. There was no more chasing my own damn tail.

Her name was Jenny Reeds.

JENNY

"Dating? Don't you have other things to worry about, young lady?"

I sighed, closing Hallie's door behind me. I'd gone in to check on her before dealing with my dad. I gestured for him to follow me to the kitchen, where I put a kettle on for tea. Then I turned to face him, bracing my arms against the counter behind me.

"Yes dad. But it's complicated."

He gave me a hard look.

"Does he know about the child?"

I stiffened. My dad had no idea that Jagger was the father. But if he did know, he would never give Jagger a chance.

"No. And I don't want to tell him yet."

My father looked at me with a look of dawning understanding.

"You already care for this young man."

I sighed.

"I do. More than I want to."

He said nothing, just stared at the table in front of him. The kettle went off and I poured us each a mug of chamomile tea. Lord knows, I could have used something stronger.

"Jenny... This is hard for me. I'm trying to think of what your mother would say."

"I know dad. Me too."

"I'd like to take that boy out back and tar his hide."

I stifled a laugh. Jagger brought that out in people apparently. But he also brought out... other things.

Tingly skin, butterflies in the tummy sorts of things.

If I wanted us to have a chance to be something real, or even just to have a little fun before he went on his merry way, I had to keep my dad from murdering him.

If nothing else, I had to keep him breathing for Hallie.

"Please don't do that, dad."

"I won't. But if he hurts you..."

"I know, I know. The firing squad, right?"

My dad's stern face cracked the teensiest bit of a smile. I put my hand over his. We were both thinking the same thing... how my mother used to tease him when he got too worked up. She'd softened him.

She'd softened us both.

I could almost imagine that she was here, stirring something on the stove behind me.

She'd listen to use argue with a wistful smile, only stepping in when one of us wasn't fighting fair. Her two mules, she'd call us. But always with a kiss or gentle hand on my shoulder.

"Well, I guess you are old enough to know your own mind."

He seemed to shake off the memories and come back to the present. Not that I wanted to. I could have lived in those memories forever.

But that wasn't life, was it? I had to deal with what was happening. With the here and now.

"Thanks dad."

He lifted his mug and stood.

"Thank you, Jenny. Goodnight."

"Goodnight."

I washed my face and brushed my teeth before crawling into bed with my tea. I was too restless to sleep so I picked up a book. Then I was too distracted to read it. I tossed and turned for a while, trying to focus with no luck.

All I could think about was Jagger.

And how I was going to explain to him why I'd kept his daughter a secret all this time.

I knew in my bones he was going to be upset when I told him.

He'd probably walk out on me for having too much baggage. But there was nothing I could do about that. Me and my girl were a package deal.

Maybe if I waited... if I gave him a chance to get to know her, and me. Maybe he'd warm up to the idea.

Maybe he'd even be glad.

I slid lower under the covers, inhaling the familiar scent of the detergent. It reminded me of my mom, even though I was the one who did the wash now.

I knew what she would tell me.

She would tell me to come clean and let the chips fall where they may. She would tell me that I was strong and I would survive with or without him. She would tell me I was a good mother and would do the right thing for my daughter and myself.

I felt tears sting my eyes as I finally started to drift off.

I wasn't so sure I was as strong as my mother after all.

9

JAGGER

"Just a little off the top. I like the sides close, though."

The barber nodded, using a spray bottle to dampen my hair. Lefoy walked in, and plopped down in the seat next to me. We'd come up in the early days together.

We hadn't liked each other much back then. People said it was because we were so much alike. He'd grown on me slightly over the years though.

Slightly.

"I heard you were back stateside, SPD."

I glanced at him, then back at my much more handsome reflection in the mirror.

"Easy on the top now."

The barber started snipping all over the top of my head. I wanted to look neat, but I wasn't looking to go back to a damn crew cut. I'd earned the right to sport a little more style.

Lefoy ran his fingers over his spikey flat top.

"Not me. I keep my shit high and tight."

"What do you want, Lefoy?"

"I want a drinking buddy. You can drink with the best of them, even if you steal all the women."

I snorted. He was worse than I was with women. Past tense.

"Not tonight my friend."

"Oh no? What's up? You got a date?"

I smiled smugly.

"Indeed I do."

"You got the bug already, doncha?"

I glared at him.

"What the hell are you talking about?"

"Guy like you, never bothering to take a lady out anywhere but your bedroom. Now all the sudden you got shined shoes and your dress uniform on. Looks like you're looking to settle down."

I said nothing. I wanted to smack him. But what he was saying was a little too close to the truth.

"Seen it happen a hundred times. Guy sees some action. Watches his friends get blown up. Next thing you know, he's itching to spawn."

He stretched and stood.

"Anyway, I'm heading down to that rib place. I saw a sweet little ginger piece of ass there the other day that would make your head spin."

He winked at me.

"Too bad you got a date."

I was out of the chair and gripping him by the collar before he could so much as blink.

"You keep your hands off her, you pig."

He held his hands up.

"Oh oh oh! Easy now, Jagger. I didn't know you had a date with little red riding hood."

I let him go, his feet settling back on the floor. He was a big guy, but I'd managed to lift him off his feet. I was so angry I could have thrown his sorry ass across the room. It made me furious hearing him talk that way about Jenny. I stepped back, willing myself to calm down.

"Just forget you ever set eyes on her."

He smiled and nodded, but I wasn't fooled. Lefoy walked to the door. Just outside he shook his head and shouted.

"She's kind of hard to forget, Jagger. I think I'll go think about little red right now- in the shower!"

He made a crude gesture in front of his crotch and took off.

I cursed and ran for the door but he was already running away like a little snake. And I was in my dress uniform. And I had a towel draped over my shoulders.

And if I took the time to properly beat his ass I was going to be late.

I could not be late for this. Especially with Lefoy sniffing around Jenny. His reputation with the ladies was almost as bad as mine.

Almost. But not quite.

I sat back in the chair and nodded at the barber. I wondered how often there were fights in the barbershop and decided to leave him a big tip for my poor manners. In ten minutes I was done and on my way to my meeting with the General. I made a quick stop at the grocery store for some flowers.

Roses. Red ones too. Like her hair. They weren't cheap either.

Women loved roses.

I walked up to the door and pressed the buzzer.

JENNY

"Up or down?"

I rolled my eyes at Crystal. Her husband had turned one of the guest rooms in their house into a salon for her to do hair. It was simple but nicely tricked out with a big mirror and a swivel chair. He'd even put in a sink and one of those chairs that leaned back for washing.

"Down. I'm not going to the prom."

She snickered.

"Were you still in high school when you... knew Jagger?"

I gave her a suspicious look in the mirror. What was she getting at anyway? I decided just to evade the question.

"No. But it wasn't long after graduation."

She made a clucking sound with her tongue. I tried to wait her out, thinking she would change the subject.

She didn't.

"What?"

She gave me a pointed look.

"You can't fool me. I saw them together, girl. I know he's her daddy."

I sighed. Of course Crystal would have figured it out. She was like a super sleuth sometimes.

She also claimed that she was psychic but I didn't believe in that kind of thing.

"Yeah. Okay."

"Does he know he shipped off with a bun in your oven?"

I shook my head quickly.

"No. We didn't... keep in touch."

"His choice or yours?"

"Mine. I mean, he said he wanted to find me but he didn't know my name. I knew his though."

"And you decided not to clue him in when you found out about Hallie?"

I nodded and she held my head still so she could work the curling iron.

"I asked around about him. And the stuff I heard... well, it made me think he wouldn't care that he'd gotten me knocked up. I felt stupid for thinking he..."

"Actually cared about you?"

It was a relief to tell someone else. Maybe she could help me figure out what to do. How to... work around the big ole elephant in the room.

"Hmmm... well, if you ask me girl, he does care. Now, anyway. I have no idea what he was like before but he is into you, no doubt."

"You think so?"

I couldn't hide the eagerness in my voice.

"Hell yes. He's smitten. I also think you better tell him ASAP, girl. I know that look."

"What look?"

"You look starry eyed."

"I do not."

"You do. You look like you are a inch from falling in love. Him too."

She pulled the curling iron through my hair again and started to fluff me.

"If you haven't already."

"I haven't! I barely... know him."

She made a rude noise and I scowled at her. Then she pulled out the hairspray. I dove out of the seat, holding my hands up.

"Keep that stuff away from me."

"Suit yourself. You will be wilting by dessert."

"I don't care. I hate that sticky stuff."

She shrugged and grumbled at me.

"Eh, you don't need any extra help anyway. Not the way you look."

"Oh, stop."

"You could wear a trash bag and look like a movie star. You hooker."

Crystal had this weird obsession with convincing me I should be a model. Or an actress. Or do something with my looks. I honestly didn't know what she was talking about.

I just didn't see it. I was plain featured and not the twig type they showed on TV, other than my hair. Sure guys made fools of themselves around me, but didn't they do that with every fertile female within spitting distance?

"Trust me, honey. Jagger doesn't stand a chance."

10
JAGGER

I stood in the living room, adjusting my stance from time to time. After ten minutes I was still waiting for the General to invite me to sit.

He didn't.

So, I just stood there. I hadn't worn my hat. But I kind of wish I had, so I had something to fiddle with.

He'd already taken the flowers, with a slightly disapproving sound. Maybe red had been a bad idea. Pink would have been better.

Red was a little too... sexual.

I stood straight, waiting. Finally, the General gestured to a chair across from him. I sat down and cleared my throat.

I noticed he hadn't offered me anything to drink either. Maybe that was a blessing. From what Jenny had texted me, it sounded like the man might try to poison it.

Hell, if I had a daughter I wouldn't make it easy for someone who wanted to go out with her either. Maybe he could sense that I wanted to steal her away from him. Maybe-

"So. You wanted to speak to me."

"Yes, sir. I wanted to let you know that my intentions towards your daughter are honorable."

Well, mostly honorable. But he didn't need to know about all the hot, sweaty things I wanted to do with her.

Tonight, if I had my wish.

"You know she's only twenty right?"

I nodded, even though I hadn't known exactly how old she was. Just that she was barely legal the first time I met her. That has been... a close call to say the least.

"Yes, sir. I won't rush her."

Not into matrimony, anyway. The other stuff, well, we'd already done that. So there was no need to delay *that* gratification.

"You like kids, Jagger?"

I nodded eagerly. This was going well. The General was actually asking me questions. And that was an easy one. I did like kids.

I'd looked after enough of them in the foster care system. The little ones were always scared, especially since plenty of foster parents were not especially nurturing.

"Dad."

I looked up to see... a vision. Jenny was standing there in a pretty, pale blue summer dress. Her hair was down and styled more than usual. She had a little bit of makeup on too. Not that she needed it.

It was just enough to let me know that she considered tonight special too.

The slight darkening of her lashes... the shimmery pink on her cheeks. It dialed her beauty up to glamorous.

I hadn't known she could look like this. She looked like a sparkling glass of pink champagne with a strawberry in it. Or the cherry on top of an ice cream sundae.

She looked like a little slice of heaven.

I gulped and stood, realizing I was in deep. Deeper than I'd thought, and I already knew I wanted her for the long haul.

Suddenly, words like 'forever' were on the tip of my tongue.

She smiled at me, then turned a cold look on her father. I smothered a laugh. Only

Jenny would look at one of the most feared men in the Marines that way.

"Are you done here?"

"Yes."

"Good."

She turned to me and her eyes softened. I wondered what her dad had done to piss her off. It was almost comical, seeing the two of them clash like that.

She held her own, and then some.

I grinned and followed her to the door.

"I brought you flowers."

She looked confused for a minute.

"You did?"

I nodded.

"He took them to the kitchen I think."

Jenny held up her finger, disappearing back into the house. She was back in a few minutes. We stepped out the door and she shut it behind us. Then she smiled at me shyly.

"Thank you. I put them in water."

She shrugged self-consciously.

"My dad wouldn't think to do it. That was always... the kind of thing my mom took care of. And since then, well..."

She smiled at me shyly.

"No one's ever brought me flowers before."

I bit my tongue, on the verge of promising to bring her flowers *every* day. I offered her my arm instead. She took it and we walked down the edge of the walkway to my ride. She stared at the gleaming black and chrome bike parked at the curb. Oh yeah, I'd polished her up for this. There were two equally shiny helmets sitting on top.

"I've never been on a motorcycle before."

I picked up the spare helmet, frowning at it.

"Your hair looks so nice... and your dress. I wasn't thinking. I'm going to call a cab. Unless... you want to ride?"

She looked at me in surprise.

"Hell yes, I do!"

She grabbed the helmet from my hand and started tucking her hair up and under it. I watched her, my mouth going a little dry at the sight of her. Her cheeks were pink. Her eyes were shining.

She was the girl I'd met all those months ago.

Almost two years now, just about. But it still felt like yesterday. She took one look at me and grinned.

"What are you waiting for? Let's go!"

I laughed and put on my helmet, then reached out to make sure hers was on securely. I inhaled sharply as my fingers brushed the incredibly soft skin under her chin. Then I climbed on the bike and pulled her up behind me.

"I won't go too fast. Not with you dressed like that."

She wrapped her arms around me.

"Don't hold back on my account, Jagger."

JENNY

I closed my eyes, loving the feel of the wind on my face. My cheek was pressed against Jagger's broad shoulder, which shielded me from the worst of it.

Of course, the wind blowing up my skirt was a different matter altogether. That was going straight up my thighs, stimulating my sensitive skin. But according to Jagger, we weren't going all that far

And despite what I'd said, *he was* holding back. I knew he was. I wondered what it was like to ride with him when he really let loose. He was being polite though. I was as inappropriately dressed for a motorcycle ride as I could possibly be.

Well... A bikini would have been worse.

I smiled at the thought of riding behind Jagger in a bright red bikini as he turned towards town. The swooping feeling was exhilarating. The cool night air was exhilarating. Jagger was the most exhilarating of all...

He pulled into the parking lot of the fanciest place in town. I was suddenly glad I'd worn one of my few dresses. Crystal's borrowed princess heels on the other hand... not the best for riding.

I was lucky one of them hadn't fallen off.

Jagger climbed off and reached for his helmet, tugging it off. I stared at him in awe. His hair still looked perfect somehow. Neat on the sides and a little bit of a party up top. I *had* to find out how he did that.

Crystal had already asked me for deets.

His blue eyes widened as he watched me tug my dress down over my thighs. He looked away politely. I almost laughed. Who was this guy and what had he done with Jagger?

"Next time, you're going to have to wear jeans."

He stepped closer and undid the strap under my chin. His fingers were gentle as he let them linger, stroking my cheek as he stared at me. My lips opened slightly, sure he was going to kiss me.

But he just stepped away and held out his hand.

I tugged off my helmet, tossing my hair to unflatten it. I grinned at him and handed it over. He took it, his eyes hungry as he looked at me.

He locked his bike up and offered me his arm to escort me into the restaurant.

In a few minutes I was sitting at a table by the window facing the back. Open French doors led to a private garden with stunning flowers. Somehow they were *all* in bloom. I realized it must take an army of gardeners to create that effect.

String lights glowed from the branches above.

A fountain was bubbling.

Along with the soft music playing inside, it was pretty much perfect.

It was definitely the most romantic thing anyone had ever done for me. Considering we'd moved around too much over the years to have a lot of friends, let alone a real boyfriend, that wasn't too surprising.

A boyfriend...

Jagger kept stealing glances at me as he read his menu. He wanted to be that I realized. My boyfriend. I took a sip of my water.

"Do you want champagne?"

I bit my lip.

"Only if you are having some."

"I can't. I'm driving you home later."

He almost said something else. I almost heard the unspoken words... much later.

"One glass then. You're a big guy. I'm sure you can handle it."

He grinned at me wolfishly. I realized he liked it when I said he was big. I blushed suddenly realizing he might think I meant his-

"May I take your orders?"

Our waiter was back. I could have sworn he had a faint French accent. We were kind of in the middle of nowhere out here though, so I kind of doubted he was from France.

Canadian maybe.

Jagger had already asked me what I wanted so he ordered for both of us. He even mentioned that I wanted my dressing on the side. I felt a little zing of pleasure at his consideration.

He was being wonderful. Kind. Romantic. Respectful. Considerate.

And I was lying to him.

That ugly reality kept intruding on my thoughts, reminding me that this was not a fairytale. And I was definitely no princess.

He started asking me about my hopes and dreams. It was hard not to mention Hallie. I almost did, twice.

"What do you want? Long term, I mean."

I shrugged.

"I guess I just want to... get away. Make enough money that I can start over somewhere new. Maybe not move every few years for once in my life."

"It must have been hard growing up on bases."

"It was different when my mom was alive. She made it seem normal. I think, in retrospect, that she must have worked really hard to do that."

"How so?"

"She always arranged our house the same way. Made sure I had my favorite books to read, and activities lined up. She even drove me back and forth to visit friends at different bases."

I shrugged.

"Mostly, I had pen pals. And my journals."

"You like to write?"

I sat up straight.

"I guess I do. I never thought of it that way... of myself as a writer. I was going to study literature in college... but I've mostly just read books. I never tried to actually write any of my ideas down."

"I'm pretty sure you could do anything you wanted to."

He didn't realize I hadn't gone to college because of our baby. I knew he would run out of here if he knew. I didn't want to ruin this perfect night. So I changed the subject.

"What about you? Where did you grow up?"

I could have sworn that Jagger's swagger dried up. He took a deep swig of his water before answering.

"I moved around a lot too."

"Army brat?"

"Not exactly."

He cleared his throat. It looked like he was having trouble meeting my eyes all the sudden.

"Foster system."

I didn't know that. It changed the way I looked at him almost instantly. He wasn't some spoiled, arrogant jerk who always got what he wanted.

But he was going to tonight.

Just like that, I knew what I wanted. I wanted *him*. I wasn't going to try and fight this crazy attraction between us anymore. I was going to just... go with it.

"Oh. What was it like?"

He shrugged.

"Some of the homes were okay. Some were... not. I ended up looking after a lot of littler kids who couldn't protect themselves."

I stared at him, my fork forgotten in my hand.

"They... hit you?"

He shook his head.

"No. Not me. But I saw a couple hit the other kids. Mostly it was that they... they didn't always feed us. And they didn't do a lot of hand holding, if you know what I mean. Some of those kids were really young. They got scared at night."

"Do you know... what happened to those kids?"

He nodded.

"Some. I am still in touch with a few of them. I had a sister I was with for a long time. We moved together twice. Until she ran away, anyway."

He smiled at me sheepishly.

"Well, I call her my sister. I'm not sure that's legit."

I stared at him, feeling the urge to reassure him. To hold him. Hell, I almost leapt over the table to sit in his lap. Instead, I just gave him a small smile.

"It's legit."

I had to look away as my eyes started to tear up. Maybe I'd been wrong. Maybe he was the daddy- type. Maybe-

"Hey, let's make a deal. Let's only talk about happy things tonight. Okay?"

I looked back at Jagger, slowly nodding. I'd been on the brink of telling him everything. Letting the chips fall where they may.

But he'd just given me an out, and I was enough of a coward to take it.

11
JAGGER

I stared at the insanely beautiful woman straddling my bike. She looked damn good on it. Hell, she looked damned good anywhere. The fancy restaurant... the bar she worked at... my bed...

I grinned at her, suppressing the hot lust coursing through me.

"So... Where to?"

She smiled at me shyly. I wasn't used to this. Both of us were pussy footing around each other. Almost afraid to ruin things.

The date was going almost *too* well. I helped her get her helmet on, tucking my jacket over her shoulders. It was getting chilly out.

"I have to get you home by a decent hour."

"Then we should go back I guess."

I nodded. I didn't want the night to be over. I wanted to keep her up all night.

Naked.

But the General was going to remove my nuts if I tried that.

"Okay, I'll take you home."

She smiled brightly at me.

"Great. I can't wait to see your place."

My eyes might have bulged out of my head. I guess Jenny misunderstood me. But I wasn't going to correct her. Or she was just as eager for me as I was for her.

And I had put fresh sheets on the bed, just in case.

Sweet Jenny was still a little bit wild after all.

My mind was racing as I drove carefully back to the base. She might just want to see my place. Maybe she didn't want to-

Her hands slid down my stomach as I pulled to a stop in front of my digs. Then she brushed my thigh. My cock lurched to attention and I moaned, hoping she couldn't hear it over the roar of the engine. I took a breath, turned the key and dismounted.

I held my helmet over my lap. It was barely big enough to cover my hard on. She looked so sweet and innocent as she got off the bike.

Then she looked me over and licked her lips.

Oh. My. Lord. Sweet, innocent Jenny *did* have something on her mind. The same thing as I did apparently. I took her hand and pulled her against me, giving into the desire I'd had to kiss her all night.

Her lips parted underneath mine and I brushed my hands over her back, then up under the jacket. My hands slid to her waist and I stopped, leaning my forehead against hers.

"We better... go inside."

She nodded and took my hand as I led her to my townhouse. I went to the kitchen as she looked around and offered her a glass of water. She accepted it, and I found myself watching her lips as she drank.

She set the glass down and we stared at each other for exactly one heartbeat. Then we were on each other, leaning against the kitchen counter as we started frantically tearing each other's clothes off. I kept kissing her, pausing for a split second as I pulled her dress up and over her head. I felt her tugging my shirt off and lifted my arms.

Our chests came together in an explosive kiss. Her bra was simple. Just a layer of thin white cotton that did nothing to hide the hardness of her nipples. I moaned as they scraped against my chest, sending tingles through my entire body. My hands reached for the back of her bra, unhooking it and sliding it over her shoulders.

I gasped at the sight of her perfect breasts. She was so beautiful, so touchable, for a moment I was not sure where to start. I kissed her again, wanting to feel those luscious globes against me. Then I bent forward, worshiping them with my mouth one at a time. Her hands were in my hair, tugging me up a few minutes later.

I hoisted her onto the kitchen counter and tore her panties off her. She whimpered as I dove head first between her thighs. Licking, and stroking and touching. She tried to close her thighs against the onslaught of sensation but I gripped them, holding them open.

I looked up at her, the question in my eyes.

"Let me."

She was out of breath, her beautiful face flushed. But she nodded. With a moan I lowered my head again and got to work, sliding my tongue up and down the line between her puffy pink lips.

She was perfect. Small, sweet, and plump. Just begging for a man's lips and tongue to taste her. And his fingers. And his cock.

Unffff...

I worked up to her clit, using my fingers to open her sweet honeyhole. I swirled my tongue against the hard little nub, fast and light. Her hips jerked.

Once.

Twice.

Three times.

And then Jenny erupted. I felt my face get wet and sticky as she creamed all over me. Her body shook so I held her down, finishing the job. She was crying out, making the sweet high-pitched noises that I remembered so well.

It was a few minutes later when I stood up, wiping my face off on the back of my arm. I stared at her hungrily, wanting to dive into her. But I didn't want to rush her. I needed her permission.

"Jenny... I'm going to lose my mind if I don't fuck you now. Please, Jenny..."

She nodded and I felt a rush of relief. I stared at her gorgeous face as I dropped my pants, tugging my cock free. I pulled a condom out of my pocket and rolled it on, my dress pants still around my ankles.

Jenny watched me, her beautiful eyes glued to my cock. I could have sworn it got even bigger, just from her staring at it. She turned me on that much.

I gripped her hips, tugging her to the very edge of the counter. Then I braced one hand against the upper cabinets behind her and slowly pressed inside her.

She was tight, almost too tight. I knew instantly she hadn't been with anyone in a long time. I didn't want to think about what she'd done while I was overseas, but I knew she hadn't dated a lot and I was fucking glad about it.

A man can tell these things.

I told her to hold on tight and I went to town.

All my manners, all my politeness was gone. I was an animal now and I was taking what I wanted.

What was mine.

My woman.

I plunged in and out of her, the suction of her sweetness keeping me from going too fast. I wanted this to last. I wanted this to-

Jenny wrapped her legs around me and locked her ankles behind my back. Then she arched against me. We were flush against each other when she started to undulate against me like a wave.

Oh fuck...

I roared and felt my cock expand. I pumped myself into her, knowing I was close. Knowing there was nothing I could do to stop it.

She bit my neck and I came, feeling her body answer mine with an orgasm of her own. She bore down on me, squeezing my cock so hard it hurt. But in a good way.

A very, very good way.

I felt my balls pulse as my seed came barreling up and out of my cockhead, pushing against the rubber blocking the way. I cursed as I drove into her again and again until I was drained.

It took a damn long time.

It had *been* a damn long time.

I leaned my forehead against hers and smiled.

There were no words to explain what had just happened between us. It had been off the charts hot. Even now, I knew I was going to have to have her again.

And soon.

The clock was ticking.

JENNY

The carpeted stairs under my back were creating static as I rubbed up against them. I could feel my hair lifting off my head in all directions as Jagger shifted my thigh to get deeper inside me. I had a pretty good feeling I was going to end up with rug burn on my ass but I didn't care.

I was insatiable for him. He was desperate for me too. It was like we were both starving and this was the only thing that would end that hunger. And we were definitely doing our best to scratch the itch.

We'd already screwed once in the kitchen.

We'd been heading for the bedroom upstairs when we'd started kissing.

We hadn't made it all the way to the second floor.

I moaned, arching my back as I started to come. I was shaking helplessly, pinned down by the hard spear of his cock. Jagger crooned soft love words to me, encouraging me to reach for it. I did.

The world shattered around me as I clung to him. We were the only two people on Earth in that moment. I held on for dear life as he rode me through my orgasm and beyond, until I was a quivering, shivering mess.

"Jenny... Oh God... Jenny..."

He was starting to lose his steady tempo. I felt him swell inside me. He was close, I could tell.

As much as I loved it when he fucked me, I loved the ending part the best. I loved making him lose control. I loved watching him come.

So I looked into his eyes. And squeezed.

Jagger shouted something garbled as his hips bucked wildly against mine. He looked like a wild man as he strained against the tide of pleasure that was washing us both away. My body started to shake with another orgasm as the energy between us zinged back and forth.

We were electric. Connected. Not just on the physical level either.

This was a spiritual experience.

I was still coming as he slowed his frantic thrusting. He stayed inside me, encouraging me to come harder, just a little bit more baby... to come for him.

I did.

I screamed as his finger brushed my clit. He was braced above me on the stairs, one hand snaking between us to toy with me. To push me over the edge, from higher than I'd ever been before. I fell, convulsing as he held me immobile with his still-hard cock.

"Jesus, Jenny... God, you are so beautiful... that's it baby... fuck, you are making me hard again."

I was panting as he started to fuck me again. I shook my head, begging for a moment to gather myself together again. He stayed inside me, slowing the tempo of his lovemaking.

"Thirsty, sweetheart?"

I nodded and he lifted his body off mine. He brought me a glass of water and I sipped it gratefully. Then he finished the glass in one long gulp.

"Come on. I think we should probably try and finish this on the bed."

"What time is it?"

He grinned at me.

"You said you had until one, right?"

I nodded, leaning on him as we climbed the stairs. He slid his hand down to my ass and squeezed.

"We have time."

The cool sheets felt like bliss after the sweaty sex we'd had on the scratchy carpeted stairs. I leaned back and he followed me down, kissing his way up my thighs.

I had a moment of panic, wondering again, what he would say when I told him about Hallie. Then I pushed it aside as he crawled up my body to kiss my lips.

Whatever this was... whatever it could be. I was going to enjoy it for as long as possible.

1 2

JAGGER

"Jenny... oh God... Fuck! We gotta stop soon."

"Hmm... keep going."

I moaned as I slid into her sweetness again and again. The first two times were quick. But this time, I was holding on with everything I had. Neither one of us wanted this to end.

But it was half past midnight. That gave us exactly thirty minutes to finish, get dressed and get her sweet little ass across town.

Hopefully not looking like she'd been fucking for three hours straight.

That... might not go over well with the General.

So yeah, we had to hurry up.

She sighed, her hips rising to meet my shaft as it embedded itself deep inside her. She was so wet that I slid right in, despite the snug fit. I was braced above her, staring down at her beautiful face as she tossed her head back and forth on the pillow.

I watched her, thinking this was pretty much the most beautiful sight on Earth.

My sweet Jenny was coming again.

That was it. I couldn't take it anymore. I gripped her hips hard as I unleashed. I came even harder this time. It reminded me of how we'd fucked all night that time before I'd shipped off.

How the condom had broke.

How amazing that happy little accident had felt.

Yeah, I'd love to go skin on skin with little Miss Jenny again. Maybe... maybe she could go on the pill or something. I'd sure as shit like to feel every inch of her creaming all over my cock again. But this was almost as good.

My whole body started shaking with the force of my orgasm. I leaned my head on the pillow next to hers as I unloaded everything I had. It was a damn lot, considering it was our third go. I rolled to the side, taking her with me.

I wanted to hold her all night. Not just tonight either. I wanted to hold her *every* damn night.

I lay there, holding her close, suddenly worried that she didn't feel the same.

But I wouldn't let that stop me. I'd make her want me back, no matter what it took. I'd take her out, charm her, woo her. She'd fall for me, just as surely as I was falling for her.

Had fallen for her. Past tense. It had happened the first damn time we met.

I kissed her and helped her get dressed. Most of our clothes were downstairs so I got the rare treat of watching her sweet hiney as it went down the stairs, her long red hair brushing her bare skin as she walked. I was grinning by the time I'd scooped her dress off the kitchen floor.

I kissed her again and again as we hurried to get dressed. It was almost like I couldn't help myself. I *had* to kiss her and touch her as much as possible. I couldn't have stopped myself if I tried.

So I didn't even bother to.

We stepped outside and she turned to me.

"How do I look?"

"Beautiful."

She sighed in relief.

"And freshly fucked."

She smacked my shoulder.

"Jagger!"

I grinned.

"I'm just kidding. You look like a beautiful..."

I kissed her hand.

"...elegant..."

I pulled her against me and kissed her lips.

"...lady."

She smiled at me.

"That's much better."

I couldn't stop myself from kissing her deeply again. Just one more time. Even though we were cutting it close.

"Come on sweetheart. Let me walk you home."

JENNY

I sighed, sitting in the rocking chair in Hallie's room. I was freshly showered and in a clean nightgown. But there was no way in hell I was falling asleep.

Jagger had pretty much blown my ever lovin' mind tonight.

He was kind and gentle and sweet and passionate... and filthy. Very, very filthy. He'd proven that when we did it. Over and over and over again.

But it was how he'd been before we got to his place that was keeping me from getting any rest tonight.

The story he'd told me about his childhood had changed everything. I could just see him, a tough but adorable little boy, looking after the other kids who needed him. He was a born protector.

I don't know why I hadn't seen it to begin with.

Well, to be honest, I had seen it. That first night together, I'd been starry eyed. Just about everything Jagger said or did had felt and seemed perfect. But I'd let those rumors about him ruin everything. I could have told him everything so long ago. I could have kept in touch, instead of just worrying if he was okay.

And I *had* worried. I'd checked the reports for his name, more often than I would ever admit to anyone. But maybe that was natural. Anyone who loved an active military man or woman, they would tell you how it was. When I was a little kid and my dad was far away, my mother and I had both gone through it.

You pretend not to worry, but it's pretty much there all the time. You had to just get up and get on with your day. But it was always there. Worrying became like breathing.

You did it every minute of every day.

That's when it hit me. I'd felt that way when he shipped off. Even after I'd heard the rumors about him.

I was in love with Derek Jagger. I think I had been, ever since that night. That crazy, perfect, unforgettable night.

I smiled at my daughter, who had been sleeping peacefully in her crib. She stretched her little hands and feet out in her sleep, her chubby legs kicking slightly as she let out a half-hearted cry. I stood and rubbed her belly gently.

That did it. She yawned and was instantly back into deep sleep again.

I stared at her, imagining that Jagger must have looked like this as a baby. I frowned, realizing he probably didn't have any baby pictures. So he wouldn't know that he looked like her

He must have been so lonely growing up... maybe he still was.

Well, other than all the female companionship he'd had.

I sighed and slipped out of the room, leaving the door open a sliver. My door was just across the hall and I'd leave that open too. I'd always been a deep sleeper, but the slightest noise from my daughter had me up and awake instantly.

It was just one of those things. I figured it must be biology at work.

Speaking of biology...

I was sore between my legs, but in a good way. My back had red marks from the runner on the stairs. But I felt good. Better than good.

I felt satisfied. Whole. Complete.

I decided not to worry about how long that feeling would last. How long before Jagger moved on to another girl. How I would tell him about his daughter.

The last thing I wanted to do was try and trap him.

If he thought I wanted him to do the right thing by me... that wouldn't be the same as if he'd stuck around on his own. I'd give him a chance to prove me wrong before I told him.

I rolled over and hugged my pillow, figuring I'd solved my problems, for now.

The ball was in Jagger's court. I'd just have to see what he did with it.

13
JAGGER

I sat on the playground bench, waiting for Jenny. We'd been on five dates over the last two weeks, all of them amazing. All of them ending in sweaty monkey sex.

Screeching, banana throwing, crazy upside down monkey sex.

Well, almost all of them.

We'd had slow, melt in your mouth, kissing all night sex too.

Except she lived with her dad, who would murder me if he knew what we were up to. So 'all night' was a stretch. But our dates had started earlier and earlier, and we'd ended up at my place earlier and earlier too.

We both wanted as much quality alone time as possible.

I walked her home from the bar each time she had a late shift too.

Basically, we were going steady.

I just hadn't gotten her to agree to it yet. Or anything really. She seemed determined not to talk about the future, or even see me during daylight hours.

So I was waiting. I was going to pin her down dammit. I wanted her by my side, ring on her finger, living under my roof.

And this was phase one of my operation.

I saw her coming and twisted to the side, hoping she wasn't going to turn tail and run when she saw me. She'd done it twice already, disappearing down another street the moment I clapped eyes on her. It was like she was a damn vampire and didn't want to see me with the sun out!

Like I'd care. I'd be in love with her even if she was a werewolf. I'd love her if she was pigeon toed or buck toothed. I didn't even care how beautiful she was anymore. Not on the outside.

Because Jenny was so beautiful on the inside, it gave me faith in humanity.

She was such a damn sweetheart, she could have looked like anyone and I would have loved her.

But every time I mentioned the L word, she cut me off or changed the subject.

Every damn time.

I was starting to wonder if I had BO or something. She didn't seem to mind being with me though. She just shied away from any serious relationship talk.

I peeked over my shoulder as she pushed the stroller into the playground. Our eyes met and she froze, her eyes wide as saucers. I jumped up and ran after her as she peeled off backwards and started pushing the stroller back the way she came.

"Jenny! Hey, wait up."

"Sorry, forgot something."

I caught up to her, practically jogging to keep up.

"What did you forget?"

"Kid needs her sunblock."

I looked at the sky. It was overcast.

"It's not even sunny today."

"Babies can burn, even on cloudy days. Need her hat too."

I tugged a pink hat out of her bag. It had been right on top. She definitely knew it was there. What the hell was going on with her?

"This one?"

She looked at it and kept going. I kept up, not ready to let her off the hook yet.

"They work you too hard."

"Who?"

"The kid's parents."

She stopped in the street and stared at me, her face looking like I'd just said something awful.

"Hey, no offense."

"It's fine. I have to go-"

"Uh uh. I need to know why you are avoiding me."

"I'm not. I saw you two days ago. And last night when you walked me home."

She chewed her full bottom lip, looking nervous.

"Thank you for that by the way. You don't have to do it every time."

I pushed her hair out of her face.

"Yes, I do."

"Jagger..."

"Why won't you commit to me, Jenny? Did I do something wrong?"

She stopped, staring at me.

"What?"

The baby let out a soft coo and I looked down at her and smiled. Then I looked back at Jenny and took her hand.

"I've been trying to talk to you about- the future- for two weeks now. You keep shutting me down."

She stared at me. Then she pulled her hand away and started walking again. Damn. This was not going well.

"I didn't think that's what you were trying to do. We can talk. Just not now."

I had to run to catch up to her again.

"Hey, where are you going?"

"Home."

"Don't you need the kid's stuff?"

She stopped again.

"Yeah. I..."

She shook her head, as if she was distracted.

"I'll see you later Jagger."

I stood there in the middle of the street, wondering if I was going crazy. Something felt off. *Really off.* I watched as Jenny walked away. I had a bad feeling in my stomach. Like she was walking away for good.

JENNY

I slammed the empty mugs down on the counter. Hard. I wanted to smash something. Break something. I wanted to-

"Easy there, Red."

Margie gave me a look, grabbing the mugs and sliding them into the sudsy water in the sink.

"Sorry."

"Something wrong?"

I shook my head and told her nothing was wrong. But that was a lie.

Something *was* wrong. For the first time, Jagger wasn't here to walk me home. My shift was almost over and the place was already shutting down.

By trying to avoid reality, I'd ruined everything.

If I'd been keeping score I would have been losing. Jagger was being so sweet to me, and I was shutting him out. Because he scared the hell out of me.

Jagger: two. Jenny: zero.

Margie dunked the soapy mugs into clean water and turned them upside down on a clean towel. It wasn't exactly sanitary, but it got the job done. I sighed and pushed the mop across the floor.

"If you're looking for Prince Charming, he's outside."

My head snapped up.

"He is?"

She nodded. Then she nodded at the mop.

"That's good enough, hon. I can finish up."

I practically tore off my apron and grabbed my purse, fishing out a compact hairbrush and lipgloss. Margie laughed, shaking her head.

"He's a good one. I'd hold onto him if I were you."

I smiled at her.

"Thank you Margie. I'm going to try."

I stepped outside to see Jagger leaning on his bike. He hadn't wanted to come in tonight apparently. I couldn't say I could blame him.

He just held out his hand and handed me the helmet. I took it, strapping it on. He didn't say a word. Neither did I.

But I didn't want him to take me home yet. I wrapped my arms around him while he straddled the bike and put his helmet on.

"I don't want to go home yet."

He glanced over his shoulder at me.

"We're going to talk, Jenny."

I rubbed my shoulder against his leather jacket in response. He started the bike and took off. This time he didn't go slow.

Maybe it's because he was upset. Maybe it's because I was dressed properly this time. Maybe it's because he didn't feel as protective of me.

But this time, Jagger went *fast*. I could still feel the tight control he had as he drove a half hour into the mountains. Up and up we went until I could smell the green and the trees and water.

There was a cool mountain lake up here. I'd never been, though Crystal and I had talked about going when the babies were a little older. I knew that's where he was taking me.

By the time he stopped, I knew I had to tell him the truth.

He got off the bike and took his helmet off, staring at me in the darkness. The moon was almost full, shining brightly on the lake. It was cool up here, not like the blazing hot sand where the base was situated. I looked around at the trees.

That was the thing I missed the most since Dad had been stationed here. The trees.

We walked towards the lake in silence, then along the shore until we found a large rock. I sat and waited. He stood there for a while, one leg up, just looking at me.

"Jenny..."

He ran his hands through his hair, staring out at the lake.

"I want to know what we are doing here. Together, I mean. If this is going anywhere."

He looked at me.

"I want it to. Do you?"

I inhaled sharply at the look in his eyes. He was open to me. No arrogance. No walls.

I tried to make light of it and failed.

"How far do you want it to go?"

He leaned forward and cupped my cheek. He was utterly serious, ignoring my lame attempt at humor.

"All the way Jenny. If you'll let me in."

I wasn't ready to hear him. To let him make me soft and vulnerable. I gave him a flirtatious look.

"I thought I already had."

He stepped back, anger darkening his eyes.

"Dammit Jenny, that's not what I mean!"

I took a deep breath. I had to take a moment to calm my heart. When I looked at him, I was serious too.

"I know."

He gave me a small, crooked smile. As if he was laughing at himself. At us.

"We are both kind of a mess, aren't we?"

I nodded.

"What was it back then? My reputation? Is that why you didn't write to me?"

I shrugged, but it felt false.

"I don't know."

That was a lie. And I was tired of lying. He deserved the truth. I sighed and looked at him.

"Yes. I heard about you and- I. I was hurt, I guess. I didn't want to be another notch on your bedpost."

He sat down beside me, turning me to face him.

"You were never that. Not from the first second I laid eyes on you."

My mouth opened. He meant it. I should tell him- I should tell him everything.

Now.

"Jagger- I have to tell you something-"

But he shook his head, putting a finger on my lips.

"Stop. I don't care what happened when I was gone. Please Jenny, don't tell me anything else. I know what I need to know."

I froze, the words fading from my lips.

"I'm in love with you, Jenny Reeds." He smiled at me, his hands gentle on my face. "And you are in love with me."

Tomorrow, I thought as he kissed me.

I'll tell him tomorrow.

14
JAGGER

I perched at the bar, leaning against it.

This was my seat. Now that we'd made it official, I was here every shift Jenny worked, the whole damn time.

I looked forward to a time when she wouldn't have to work here. When she'd be home by my side at night. But for now, it was kind of fun to watch her make fools of dozens of men, night after night.

She was doing something different tonight though. Jenny was using her feminine wiles deliberately for once. Tonight, she was messing with *me*.

Jenny was deliberately and purposefully teasing the hell out of me.

And it was working.

I knew she was getting even with me. That it might have something to do with the fact that I wouldn't sleep with her the night at the lake. And I hadn't been keeping her out past eleven any night since. I didn't want to piss off her old man.

Not when I was planning on asking for her hand.

Now she was getting her revenge. She was driving me absolutely nuts with her flirtatious glances and swaying hips. I knew, without a doubt, that I'd be giving her what she was after before dropping her home tonight.

Tonight, the General was going to have to wait a little longer to say goodnight to his little girl. Hell, the way I was feeling, I was tempted to keep her out until dawn. I could easily have found things to do with her till then.

I sipped my beer, watching her as she served a table full of army guys.

The prim country blouse of hers was unbuttoned a little farther than usual. Something lacey and pink peeked out at the bottom. Some sort of fancy lingerie I'd never seen before.

Every time she bent over to get something, she arched her back. Just a little. Just enough to make those curves of hers even more pronounced.

She slid her eyes over to me now and then, to gauge my reaction. I stared at her, rubbing my fingers over my lips. I hadn't planned on stopping at my place tonight after her shift, but now there was no choice.

I was hard as a rock, and rapidly overheating.

She knew it too, from the way she grinned at me, letting her eyes slide down my body. I was angled towards the bar, mostly to hide the massive erection she was giving me.

She grinned and flounced away, that high, heart shaped ass of hers bouncing justttt enough to draw every eye in the place. Jenny's sweet ass was that rare combination of firm and soft at the same time. The perfect handful to grab onto when doing your business.

And unlike any of the jackoffs staring at her and drooling, *I* actually knew that from experience.

"Damn, that's a fine ass. Am I right?"

My eyes cut to the guy standing at the bar beside me. He was Army. I could tell with just a glance. Our two branches of the Armed Forced did not mix well.

Never mind the fact that he was oogling my woman like she was a piece of meat. She chose that moment to slide behind the bar and smile at me. She saw the asshole next to me and froze.

"Hi Jenny."

"Oh, hi Davis. How are you?"

Great. She knew him. I said a silent prayer.

Please God do not let him be her ex-boyfriend.

The thought of his hands on her,.. well, it would be hard for me to get that thought out of my head. I said nothing, just sat there biding my time.

"Please sweetheart, call me Clyde."

The guy was oilier than a rattlesnake. I felt my nails bite into my palm and I unconsciously made a fist. Jenny didn't look too happy at the guy's cloying tone either.

Definitely not an ex-boyfriend then. I smiled. That made me love her just a little bit more than I already did.

My girl had taste. Not like some women who preened no matter who came near them. Or try to make their man jealous just for the attention.

Jenny's flirtatious manner shut down instanfuckingtaneously. I smiled at her and she gave me a cute little smile. Then she shut it down again.

"What time do you get off from this dive anyway?"

Jenny gave him a cold stare and answered Margie, who told her to bus some pretty clean looking tables. Jenny left with a clean rag and a tray without saying a word. Margie on the other hand, had plenty to say.

She leaned against the bar and gave Davis a look that would freeze lava.

"Dive, eh?"

Clyde had the presence of mind to look uncomfortable. But that didn't stop him from being a shit heel.

"That's what it is, isn't it?"

Margie gave him a cold look, using her rag to knock his beer off the counter. He jumped back as his shirt got splattered. The glass had been nearly full. She just smiled at him, looking kind of like a pirate.

"Nope. It's a juke joint."

He gave her an incredulous look and she turned away. I was hiding a smile as he used napkins to blot his shirt. He held his hands out to the side, staring at his wet button down shirt.

"Shit. Hey, can I at least get another beer *please?*"

Margie nodded.

"Sure, honey. I'll be there in a bit. Customers."

She waited on every single person at the bar, sliding them free drinks even if their glasses were full. After twenty minutes she tossed a beer at David who was fuming at that point. He caught it in mid-air I'd been hoping it would smash his head.

He twisted the cap off without thanking her. He just turned to watch Jenny working. He wasn't even subtle about what he was looking at.

It wasn't her face.

Yeah, I'd had just about enough.

"Maybe you haven't heard, jackass, but she's off the market."

He barely spared me a glance. He was too busy pulling on his drink and oogling my woman. I felt the urge to beat his ass ratchet up a notch.

"Oh yeah? Says who?"

I stared at him.

"She does."

He finished his beer and turned back to Margie. His voice was dripping with sarcasm as he sneered. "I'll take another one, *honey*." He used the same term of endearment she had. He didn't know that Margie only talked like that when she hated you.

If she actually liked you, she was salty as fuck.

She just nodded and he turned away, back to watching Jenny. This time I didn't mind so much though.

Because he didn't see Margie spit in it.

Feldon walked in with a few of his buddies. I took another beer from Marge, who refused to let me buy myself drinks anymore. The woman had a big heart, even if she cursed like a sailor.

"Jagger!"

I nodded to Feldon and lifted my beer. I looked around but the meat puppet had slithered off thankfully. It took me a couple of minutes to realize that neither he or Jenny were in the room.

"Motherfucker."

JENNY

I was bent over in the stock room, sorting empties into a case. As soon as I filled one up, I added it to the stack by the back door. Then I started on the next.

"You shouldn't lift that. Too heavy for you, cutie."

I twisted, looking behind me. Clyde stood there, his eyes looking glazed over. I got a chill, wondering why I hadn't noticed how damn *creepy* he was.

His head was tilted in a way that made it very obvious he'd been trying to get the best view of my ass. He was craning his neck, practically upside down. I turned back to what I was doing, ignoring the feeling of his eyes on me.

I still had work to do.

"You shouldn't be back here, Davis. No customers."

I felt him behind me, an instant before his hands closed over my ass. For a second I was shocked. Then a fury unlike any I had ever known flashed through me.

The fuckwit had *no idea* what he'd just done.

I twisted, still in a crouch. Then I brought my arms together to wrap one hand over the fist. Then I swung up.

Kinda like I was playing volleyball.

I was pretty sure I heard a crunch as my fist connected with his sac. I jumped back, already wanting to wash my hands. I didn't want to touch him *at all*, even though it was satisfying to watch the stupefied look on his face turn into a grimace of pain.

I was too angry to be satisfied with that though. I wanted to punch his stupid face. His stupid, *furious* face. His normally placid features twisted into something ugly as he snarled at me.

"Fucking bitch!"

"You shouldn't have touched me, Davis. Now get out."

He stood up, clearly still in pain. He loomed over me. He was big. Suddenly, I felt like I might be in trouble.

Big, bad trouble.

"Fuck no. Not until you lick my sac and make it feel better."

"You're disgusting!"

"And you're a cheap tramp!"

He grabbed me and I flailed, trying to twist away from him. I started to panic as his hands closed over my arms. He was too strong. His hands were all over me as I struggled. I cursed, realizing I was going to have to scream for help. I didn't have my damn pepper spray or my taser.

He was fucking lucky about that. I'd really like to tase his balls.

I screamed but he covered my mouth. No one was coming to help me. He couldn't do this. Couldn't get away with this-

"Guess I could just fuck you and leave you with another illegitimate baby, you whore."

I hadn't seen Jagger come into the stockroom. But I saw his face as he grabbed Davis's shoulder and yanked him off me. I'd never seen Jagger's face like that. It was a mask of cold, hard fury.

Relief mingled with panic as the two huge men faced each other. I was suddenly afraid again. I knew that look on Jagger's face.

Things were about to get ugly.

Jagger paused and flashed a look at me. He wasn't waiting for Davis to steady himself. He was waiting for me to get out of

the way. I stumbled backwards, leaning against the shelves by the back door.

Then all hell broke loose.

Jagger's fists started flying, so fast they were almost a blur. He'd inadvertently given Davis time to recover but it wasn't enough to even the odds. Davis wasn't as fast as Jagger and he definitely wasn't as pissed off.

And then it happened.

Jagger flipped the switch to combat mode. He was practically vibrating with his anger less than a minute before. But now he had an incredible control of himself.

My boyfriend's fists were a blur as he pummeled Davis, forcing him backwards. I got out of the way in a hurry, darting across the room to the other corner. Jagger was so calm that he actually turned and looked at me, mid-punch.

"You okay?"

Davis's head had snapped back. But he saw his opening and took it. I screamed but it was too late.

"Look out!"

Davis had sucker punched him. Jagger's whole body turned with the punch, going with the momentum to minimize the damage. But I knew it was going to leave a mark.

With a roar Clyde jumped on him but Jagger was ready. They wrestled, knocking over boxes left and right. Davis broke free and they circled each other, both of them wary. They had each other's measure now. It was almost an even match.

Almost.

But Jagger was just a little bit crazier than Davis. A little bit stronger too. And he'd seen more action. He knew how to handle himself in a high-pressure situation.

Davis on the other hand, was a weak bellied jackass.

He hit Davis again and again, punctuating the hits with ground out words. Davis was in a defensive position now, unable to do anything but try and block the punches.

He wasn't being too successful at that either.

"Never."

Jagger's fist hit his gut.

"Touch."

Jagger's elbow snapped Davis' chin up.

"Her."

166

He pulled his fist back and drove it straight into Davis' nose.

"Again!"

We all heard the crunch. Davis bent forward, covering his face as blood gushed out of his badly broken nose. He was squealing like a pig.

Jagger grabbed him by the collar and forcibly carried him to the back door. I opened the heavy metal door and Jagger tossed him through it. Davis landed on his side, still covering his face with his hands. He stared up at us, sprawled on the ground by the dumpster.

"You broke my nose, you bastard!"

Jagger leaned out the door, spitting blood inches from Davis's prone body.

"Good."

He wiped his lip off and smiled coldly.

"If you see her out, cross the street. Don't speak her name. Don't even look at her."

His voice was cold and his look unflinching. If I were Davis, I'd be peeing my pants right about now. Actually, Davis looked like he might.

"Next time I won't be so nice."

Then he looked at me. I watched as Jagger slammed the door and locked it. I ran into his arms and he held me tight, kissing my hair. Then he pushed me away, looking carefully at my face.

"Are you alright, Jenny?"

"Yes. I'm fine. Are you alright?"

He ignored my question, running his hand over my face. Like he was making sure I was real.

"Did he hurt you?"

"He just... pawed at me a little bit."

"I wanted to kill that bastard for touching you. I really did."

He crushed me against his chest again. I felt so safe. So protected.

So loved.

Then Jagger stumbled on his feet. I cursed, realizing he was in worse shape than he'd let on. He'd won the fight, but he'd taken a lot of hits in the process. He was hurt.

I helped him sit on a case of beer and looked him over.

"Did you ride?"

He shook his head and pointed at his boots.

"Nope. I used my feet."

I rolled my eyes. He was loopy alright. At least he wasn't feeling any pain. Not yet, anyway.

"Come on champ, I'll take you home."

Margie's eyes were wide as we came out of the stockroom. Jagger was leaning on me. Not hard, but he was weaving around a bit.

"Sorry Margie. There's a mess in the back."

She leaned on the bar.

"You take out the trash, Jagger?"

He nodded and she smiled big and wide.

"Don't you worry about a thing then. You two go on home."

She tossed him a cold bottle of beer and he caught it.

"For your cheek."

He toasted her and held it against his face as we stumbled out and into the cool night air.

15
JAGGER

I watched Jenny as she organized her supplies on the kitchen counter. I was sitting on a stool, slowly bleeding onto the linoleum. She looked so beautiful, so precious to me. Even though the scuffle with Davis had messed up her hair and torn the shoulder of her shirt.

The thought of what he'd tried to do made me sick. It made me see red. It made the pain far away, a minor concern.

Something else was bothering me though. Something Davis had said to her when he thought they were alone. It was fuzzy but I couldn't stop thinking about it.

"What did he mean?"

"What?"

I winced as she dabbed peroxide on my swollen cheek. He'd split it with that sucker punch, just a little. Just enough to leave a scar. That thing he'd said was itching at the back of my mind though.

It hadn't made any sense at all. I stared at her, feeling like I was looking through carnival glass at a stranger. Something wasn't right.

"Davis. What did he mean about giving you a baby?"

She looked at me. Then she went back to what she was doing.

"He's disgusting. I can't believe I used to think he was a nice guy."

"Yes, but Jenny. What did he mean? He said *another* baby. Didn't he?"

"What do you think he meant? He was being a pig."

I just looked at her, waiting. She finished cleaning my cheek and leaned back. She bit her lip, suddenly looking very, very nervous.

"Jenny? What is it?"

She took a deep breath, then got some antibiotic ointment and a gauze bandage. She applied it and taped the soft white square to my cheek.

"I don't need all that."

"Just leave it on tonight. Please?"

I nodded and waited. I was waiting for her to tell me the truth, though I was already starting to suspect it. I needed to hear it from her though. The picture was coming into focus. I couldn't believe how stupid I'd been. How blind.

Jenny wouldn't look at me while she started to clean up. But at last she started to talk.

"I'm not a babysitter."

My voice was thick. From emotion or being punch drunk, I couldn't say.

"What do you mean?"

She exhaled and looked at me. She looked nervous. She was afraid to tell me.

"I have a kid, Jagger. Hallie is mine."

I nodded. It made sense. It explained why she'd waited to go to school. And the wistful way she talked about going back to college someday. It explained her ferocious work ethic.

And why her father had asked me if I liked kids.

"Why didn't you tell me?"

She was staring at the floor, the wall, anywhere but at me.

"At first I thought you would run. That we were just having fun, and that if I told you, it would ruin it."

She looked at me.

"Everything I'd heard about you. Everything I thought you were. I thought that was the last thing you would want."

I swallowed, getting a very strange feeling in the pit of my belly.

"I won't run. I don't care who you were with before. As long as you're with me, now."

She looked away and I knew- I knew before she even said anything that she was about to crush me.

And then she did.

Her eyes were shining as she lifted them to mine.

"That's just the thing, Jagger. I wasn't with anyone else."

I stared at her, uncomprehending.

Then I got it. *I got it.* I closed me eyes, one thought running through my head over and over again.

"You mean-"

"You're her daddy."

I was a father. Me. The wildest fixed-wing pilot to serve in a decade. The never-settling-down type. The eternal bachelor.

I was a daddy.

The first thing I felt was happiness. Pure, shining and bright. Jenny and I had a baby. Together.

Then it hit me. She hadn't told me. The kid was - what - almost a year old? I'd missed out on all of that time. I hadn't gotten the chance to be there for her.

For either one of them.

"What the fuck, Jenny?"

"I'm sorry Jagger. I... didn't expect to fall in love with you."

"You should have told me! Right fucking away!"

I stood up and started pacing. I was furious. How could she keep this from me? I could have come home for the birth of our child. I could have been involved. But- she hadn't wanted me.

So I'd missed *everything*.

She was wringing her hands, fighting back tears. I'd never seen her so upset. I'd never seen her be anything but strong.

Normally, I would comfort her. But right now, I didn't fucking care. I was too angry.

And what she said next made me so angry I couldn't even look at her.

"You don't have to- do anything. I don't expect you to support her- or us. I never wanted to make you feel responsible. It was my choice to... keep her."

I forced my breathing to slow down. I felt like I was in combat, my heart was racing that fast. I was so angry that I took a step away from her, afraid to be too close.

If she touched me, I knew I would shatter.

"Are you shitting me? I'm not responsible? *For my own child?*"

She took a step towards me, reaching out with her hand.

"You could be- if you wanted to. I was always going to tell you, Jagger. I just-"

"You have a lot of fucking nerve, Jenny."

"I- what?"

JENNY

"You kept her from me. Even after I told you I didn't have a family."

Jagger was staring at me with clear cold eyes. He'd been confused at first. Then upset.

Now he was full on furious.

No, he was past furious. He looked at me like I was a stranger. Like he hated me.

"You kept my daughter from me."

"If I thought you would have wanted her- or us- I would have-"

"Shut up!"

He held his head in his hands, leaning against the wall. I could see he was trying to wrap his head around it. Trying to calm himself down.

"I don't understand. Are you saying that you want her? You want our little girl?"

He didn't look at me when he nodded.

"Yeah, Jenny. I fucking want our little girl."

He looked at me and I took a step back from the withering ice in his gaze.

"But I'm not sure I want you."

My jaw dropped.

"Because I didn't tell you?"

"You lied to me. You lied to me and you used me."

"Please Jagger... let me explain. Let me-"

I reached out to touch him but he flinched away.

"No! I can't talk to you. I can't even look at you."

"Why?"

The word was torn out of my chest, leaving a huge gaping hole full of pain. He laughed bitterly, still leaning his hands on the wall.

"You truly believed I would abandon a child. After what happened to me. After everything I told you."

He looked at me then. And I knew it. I felt it in my gut.

I'd lost him.

"You don't know me at all, Jenny."

I gripped the kitchen counter, wishing that this was a dream. A dream I could wake up from. But it wasn't. I'd hidden from the truth and now it was here, destroying everything in its path.

Destroying *us*.

"I tried to tell you! So many times!"

"You should have tried *harder*."

I choked back a sob. I would not cry. Not when it turned out he did want our little girl. I'd been so stupid. So wrong.

And now I was losing him.

"You can see her anytime you want, Jagger. I would never- never try to keep you from..."

But I had. I had deprived him of the chance to prove me wrong. To watch her grow up.

To love her.

He was watching me coldly. A bitter smile was on his lips. As if he knew what I was thinking.

"I think you should leave."

I nodded jerkily, grabbing my purse and walking towards the door on wooden legs. He watched me go then he followed me out onto the street. I realized that in his twisted way, he was being a gentleman. For the last time ever, he was walking me home.

The whole way across the base, I was fighting back tears. Trying to hide them. But I shouldn't have worried. He never came close enough to see me cry.

He walked half a block behind me. I glanced over my shoulder as I walked up my front path. He stood there in the street, looking broken.

I wanted to hold him. To tell him I was sorry. I wanted to beg for his forgiveness.

Instead, I put my key in the lock, and turned it.

When I looked back, he was gone.

16
JAGGER

I stared at the ceiling, thanking God that it was the weekend. Not that I had a lot to be grateful for. Not after I'd thought I found someone who loved me as much as I loved her.

What a joke.

She saw me as a playboy. Someone to pass the time with. Someone for fun.

Meanwhile, I'd been planning to spend the rest of my life with her.

I rubbed my face. I would have to see her. If I was going to be in the kid's life.

Not the kid. A daughter. *My daughter.*

Hallie...

I closed my eyes, trying to pull up every time I'd seen her. I'd thought she was a remarkably pretty child. No surprise there, considering the gene's Jenny had passed down to her.

But... mine too. Somewhere in that sweet baby girl, was a touch of Derek Jagger.

Maybe more than a touch. Maybe a whole hell of a lot.

I shook my head. I was a father. And I wasn't going to be an absentee one either. That meant I'd have to see Jenny. Watch her with someone else eventually.

Someone she considered worthy.

Unlike me.

I didn't think I could bear it to tell the truth. But then I thought about that little baby. Her eyes had been aqua. As if you'd mixed my blues with Jenny's greens.

So beautiful it made my insides twist up.

I couldn't wait to hold her. I grimaced as I rolled over. I was sore from the fight. I'd been up half the night, trying to drink away the memories. But thanks to all my years in the military I'd been up at the crack of dawn, feeling lower than the lowest scumbag on the planet.

Jenny didn't think I was good enough. Not for more than playing around. I was just... a stud to amuse her.

I rolled over, moaning at my sore ribs. My phone was on silent. She'd called and texted me numerous times.

They all said the same thing.

I'm sorry. I'm so sorry.

I shook my head. She wasn't sorry. She was not the girl I'd thought she was. She might be brave and beautiful- raising a kid alone was hard. I knew that.

It's not like she gave it up.

But... she'd lied. And lied and lied and lied.

Even as I wanted to reach for the phone, to tell her I forgave her, to tell her to come over so I could kiss her and hold her and bury myself inside her beautiful body and never come out again... Even as all that welled up inside me, I knew it wouldn't work.

No matter how good we were together in bed, that one fact would remain.

She didn't think I was good enough.

And nothing on Earth could change her mind.

Maybe if I proved to her I could be a good dad... if I showed up early every single time it was my turn. Bought the kid lots of presents and new stuff. Taught her to ride her first bike... maybe then Jenny would see that I could be good enough for Hallie.

For both of them.

Even as I started to get excited about that idea, I knew that it was wrong. I *would* be a good dad. But I wouldn't do it for her.

I'd do it for Hallie.

The rest of it, well, the chips would fall where they may.

There was only one person I could talk to about this. One person who would understand how I felt. I picked up my phone, flinching at the number of missed calls and called Suzy.

JENNY

I bent down, sweeping the broken glass off the floor of the stock room. I hadn't slept at all last night. Mattress rattling sobs tend to keep a girl up all night. But I had still peeled myself off the bed this morning, looked after my daughter and headed in to work.

I couldn't leave the mess from the fight for someone else to clean up.

It was my mess. And I was taking responsibility for all of it.

Margie walked in, leaning against the doorway with her arms folded.

"You look terrible."

"I know. I'm... sorry about all of this Margie."

She shook me off.

"Think nothing of it. It's a bar. Fights happen."

She helped me finish cleaning the stock room. Then she flicked her head and told me to take a seat at the bar.

"Now. Tell me what's wrong."

I took a shaky breath. In and out Jenny. I was scared though. I knew saying it out loud would make it more... real.

"Jagger broke up with me."

She made a snorting sound.

"I don't believe it. That man is head over nuts in love with you."

I shook my head.

"He won't even answer my calls, Margie."

"Seriously?"

"Seriously."

She stared at me, frowning.

"What the hell did you do? Another man? That don't seem like you, honey."

"No. Something... something worse."

Her eyebrows shot straight up. Then she pulled out two shot glasses and a bottle of tequila and set them on the bar. She poured us each a shot and handed me one.

"Drink."

I drank. Hallie would get formula tonight. It wouldn't hurt her. The doctor had said it was fine to mix it up. I was so numb that I was barely thinking or feeling at this point.

"Now talk."

"I- I have a kid. A little girl. Her name is Hallie. She's ten months old now."

She poured us another drink and we tipped it back. The liquid burned my throat. I wanted to feel the sting of it though. I felt myself start to loosen up.

"And?"

"I didn't tell him."

"Okay. That's not great, but not break up bad."

I looked at her.

"I didn't tell him... that Hallie was his."

She poured me another drink. I sipped this one.

"I'm sure you had your reasons. Stupid reasons. But reasons."

"I'm an idiot. I thought... I thought he was going to hurt me. So I just..."

"Lied."

"Evaded."

She shook her head.

"No, honey. You lied."

This time I reached for the bottle and refilled my glass. My phone started buzzing and I leapt for it. But it was only Crystal. I told her where I was and Margie said to invite her over.

That's how three drunk redheads ended up sitting at a bar at two o'clock in the afternoon.

It sounded like the start of a dirty joke, but it was my life. And they were my friends. And I was more grateful than ever for them.

Even though they didn't let me off the hook for a second.

"You really fucked up, girlina."

Crystal tipped back her drink, biting down on a lime wedge. She'd already licked the salt off her hand.

Yep, we'd evolved all the way to lick it, slam it, suck it. Margie was swaying a little on her feet.

"I told you to tell him."

Margie looked at her.

"Wise woman. I like her."

Crystal grinned at her.

"I like you too. I'd love to get my fingers on your hair..."

I rested my spinning head on my arms. The bar was starting to tilt in an unfortunate way. I knew I'd pay for it later but I didn't care.

At the moment, I felt all floaty, even though I was still fucking sad. It was an improvement over Earth bound and ass backwards. Hell, anything would be an improvement.

But this wasn't going to last. Soon, I'd be sober. And I'd still be alone.

"What am I going to do?"

"You're going to get your man back."

"How?"

Crystal smiled at me.

"First, a makeover."

I rolled my eyes at her. But Margie was the one with the first realistic suggestion. She toasted me with a shot.

"Then, you beg."

17
JAGGER

I brushed my hair back off my forehead with my hand. I was standing outside Jenny's house, sweating bullets. This was an important day and I was nervous as fuck about it.

I was here to get my girl for an afternoon out.

The little one.

The door opened and I inhaled sharply as my eyes nearly bugged out of my head. Jenny stood there in a red dress. A very, very tight dress. It was very short and very low cut. I could see everything I'd been dreaming about since we split up. All those luscious curves of hers. Those gorgeous legs of her wobbled a bit in a pair of four-inch stilettos.

Also red.

She looked like a super model in a music video. Sex on wheels. Hell, she looked so hot she might burn my eyes out.

But in a good way.

She tugged at the neckline self-consciously, before giving me an overbright smile. She looked beautiful of course. But weird. Almost too good. Like she was an actress, playing herself in a movie.

I realized she was wearing eyeliner. And lipstick. Red, shiny lipstick. I stared at her lips hungrily, wondering why she was dressed like that. Was she going on a date? Or was it,.. for me?

I felt myself wanting to toss her over my shoulder and carry her back to my cave. I wanted to ask her where she was going. No- I wanted to *tell* her where she was going. *My bed.*

I shut it down.

No Jagger. She's off limits. Don't be the manwhore she thinks you are. Just because your dick is like a missile that wants to explode on her... Just because looking at her and not touching her makes you want to curl up in a ball and cry... well, it doesn't change a damn thing.

Today was about Hallie and that was it.

I forced myself to look away from the gorgeous woman in front of me. I looked behind her instead. There, in a stroller, was an adorable little angel.

My angel.

I knelt down as Jenny rolled her out to the front stoop.

"Hi there."

Hallie gurgled at me, her eyes shining brightly. She... she did look like me. Me and Jenny. I wanted to look up at her. To hold her hand and thank her for giving me such a beautiful child.

If nothing else, she gave me this tremendous gift.

But I didn't.

"Thanks for letting me see her."

I made my voice and face cool as I finally glanced up at her. Jenny was watching us, tears in her eyes. She looked broken.

"Of course. Anytime you want to-"

I felt my throat tighten. Jenny was being good about this. She could have told me to go to hell after I broke it off with her. I didn't have a legal leg to stand on and we both knew it. So yeah, she was being more than fair. That didn't surprise me. She was a good woman. She was a *good person.*

But that didn't change the facts.

I held onto them, repeating them in my head. She didn't think I was a good enough person to be a dad. She'd thought I would run off, or leave them. She'd thought I was *that guy.*

No matter how she looked at me, with love and regret in her eyes, deep down she thought I was a piece of trash. And I'd thought she was the most perfect woman in the world.

There was no balance there. And I'd decided I wasn't going to do that to myself. I'd never be good enough for her.

I wasn't going to let myself feel like that just to be with her. Even if I got to hold her at night. For how long would she deign to let me touch her?

Until someone better came along.

I stood up and cleared my throat.

"I'm looking forward to getting to know my daughter."

I grabbed my purse and waited. He paused.

"Alone."

I stared at the ground. I couldn't look at him. I felt ridiculous; standing there in the four-inch heels Crystal had forced me to wear.

"Sure. Right. Okay."

Crystal was leaning in the hallway behind me. She'd come out when she realized it wasn't going so well. Watching the Titanic sink, more or less. She volunteered to go with them but I shook my head.

"That's okay. He has a right to take her."

Now Jagger shook his head. He didn't want my trust. He'd made it clear he didn't trust me.

"It's okay. I don't mind a chaperone."

He didn't mind if someone went with them. Just not me.

"No."

I wiped my eyes, hoping he didn't notice. He wasn't even looking at me anyway.

"She gets sleepy around four. And here-"

I handed him her diaper bag. Our fingers brushed and I felt a jolt. I wondered if that would be the last time I ever touched him. Maybe I'd have a handshake to look forward to someday in the future. How pathetic. He flinched away from me like he'd been burned.

"There's um, a bottle in there with a little bag of ice to keep it cool. Diapers and her hat. Just keep her out of the sun..."

"Got it. Anything else?"

"No. Just... call if you need anything."

"See you at four."

"Okay. See you."

I couldn't look at him until he'd turned away. I was afraid to see that look in his eyes again. That look that was like we didn't mean anything to each other. Like we never *had* meant anything to each other.

Like I was a stranger.

Crystal came up behind me and reached forward to slowly shut the door. I covered my mouth with my hand and turned away, running for my bedroom. I couldn't hold back another second. I cried harder than I'd cried in years.

Almost as hard as I had after my mom was gone.

"I can stay. Or come back to do the trade off at four so you don't have to-"

I nodded, crying too hard to answer. Crystal gave me a sympathetic look and shut the door. I curled up on the bed, crying so hard my whole body shook.

I didn't move the entire time he was out with her. Crystal came back twenty minutes before he was due back. She took one look at me and shook her head.

I forced myself to take a quick shower and started making Hallie's dinner of mushed up sweet potatoes. I stayed in the kitchen when the doorbell rang. I stayed there, hiding, though I could hear the low murmur of his voice.

I heard the door shut and a moment later Crystal was giving my baby back to me. I gripped her tightly, inhaling her scent. I thought I could smell a little bit of him too.

This was the only thing that was right.

My beautiful baby girl was all I had.

Even with my friends, and my dad, I was alone.

18

JAGGER

"Does she always dress like that?"

"Stop it, Suze."

My foster sister sat on my kitchen counter, flicking things at me while I tried to clean the kitchen. She'd waited a block away while I picked up Hallie yesterday so she'd seen the outfit. Suze was here for the weekend, helping me get ready. I'd bought a bunch of baby stuff at the store today.

I'd even gotten some real furniture for the place.

You needed a dining table to go with a high chair after all.

"What? The girl breaks your heart and has the gall to look like a fucking supermodel?"

She shook her head.

"You sure know how to pick 'em, bro."

"She's not like that."

"What? Vain? No woman looks like that by accident dude."

Suzy prided herself on being a tomboy. She wore a fringed leather jacket and beat up jeans. She'd never worn heels in her life. She was gorgeous actually, but she made sure she never looked like she was trying to be.

I knew she'd had her share of rough times that made her not want to encourage male attention. She didn't talk about it, but I knew something had happened to her before we met. She was as ferocious as me when protecting the younger foster kids back in the day.

"I don't know why she was dressed like that. She's usually... not. "

I scrubbed a little harder and Suze hit the back of my neck with her bottle cap.

"Bullshit."

"Ow! Christ. I'm telling you, she's usually in jeans and a button down. I bet it was her best friend's idea. She's a hairdresser or something."

"Now that I believe. The post break up makeover is a classic chick move. Well, brother, if you want that girl back you better get in line. She's got to have guys on the back burner."

"She doesn't. Besides, it doesn't matter. I don't want her back."

"Liar. You don't just fall out of love with someone. Even if they fuck up. And this was a monumental fuck up."

I sighed and rubbed my neck. Suze was right of course. I was still in love with Jenny. How could I not be?

"She doesn't deserve you, of course. No mortal woman does, Still, must have been hard, having that baby all by herself. How old was she anyway?"

I flinched. I knew she was right. I couldn't stop thinking about it either. Jenny must have been so scared. And pissed at me for knocking her up.

Even more so when she found out my reputation...

I'd tried to imagine her telling the General. That must have been a gut wrenching conversation.

But she could have told me. She could have had my support, even from overseas. I would have done anything for her, or the baby.

Hell, I still would.

But she didn't know that. She couldn't have. She was barely eighteen years old and so proud...

"Fuck."

Suze toasted me, swigging her beer and belching.

"Yes, you *are* fucked. Get me another beer."

The doorbell rang and I shook my head.

"Get it yourself."

I opened the door and froze.

Jenny was standing outside in the rain. No umbrella. She was soaked. The sheerness of her shirt clung to her curves in a way that made my mouth dry and my fingers itch to touch her.

Hell, I wanted to do more than touch her. I wanted to fuck her senseless.

But I wouldn't.

Not after what she'd done.

She didn't look like a heartbreaker though. She looked heartbroken. Just a lost little girl standing in the rain. I felt myself soften towards her again. Each day, each time I thought about it, I let my guard down just a little bit more.

"Can we talk? Please?"

I stared at her, knowing that if I let her in now, I wouldn't ever stop loving her. Maybe I was doomed. I knew she would be able to hurt me any time she wanted.

It didn't matter though. I couldn't leave the woman I loved standing outside in the pouring rain. I stepped to the side, about to tell her to come in when her eyes shot to something over my shoulder.

"Turk Jagoff- all you have is- cans..."

Suze let *her* voice trail off, staring at Jenny standing in the door. I looked at Jenny and saw the hurt in her face. I knew what she was thinking.

I knew how it looked.

She took off at a run.

"Jenny!"

I was barefoot but I ran after her anyway. She was too fast though. She darted between the houses and I lost sight of her.

I had a feeling I'd just lost more than that.

JENNY

"Now? You're leaving now?"

I shoved another baby blanket into our luggage. We had two bags, Hallie and I. Two bags, my purse, a stroller and a couple thousand bucks.

And that was it.

It was just going to have to be enough.

"Margie has a cousin with a place in Charleston. She said she'd put in a good word. Said I had a job waiting for me."

I paused, looking at Crystal.

"*Probably* waiting for me."

"Where the hell are you going to live?"

I shrugged.

"I'll find a place. Even if I have to stay in an SRO for a few days-"

"An SRO? Hell, to the no girl."

I ignored her, choosing between my few pairs of jeans. I didn't have room for much so I picked the neatest pair. The ones I'd be wearing to job interviews.

God help me if someone wanted me to wear a suit or something.

My eyes fell on the letter I'd spent hours agonizing over. It was already in an envelope. His name was neatly written on the front. I picked it up gingerly, like it was a bomb that might go off.

"Can you... can you give this to Jagger? Not today. Or tomorrow. Just... eventually. Or if he comes looking for me."

"You're really running out on him? Again?"

I shook my head.

"He's already moved on, Crys. And it's not a love letter. It's a promise that he can see his daughter. I just need to get a lawyer to draw up some paperwork."

"I don't believe it. That man is crazy in love with you."

"No. Maybe he was. But... well, that's over now."

"I don't think so. I was there, girl. I saw the way his eyes popped out of his head when he saw you in that dress."

I tried to keep my voice light. To not let on how humiliating that moment had been. I had cringed a thousand times when I remembered it. The way his eyes had skittered away from me. He hadn't been turned on.

He'd been embarrassed for me.

"He thought I looked ridiculous, Crys. No offense."

"None taken. But trust me, ridiculous was not what he thought."

I held my hand out and she took the envelope with a heavy sigh.

"Fuck. I'm going to miss you, Red number two."

"You too, Red number one."

I smiled at her tremulously. I couldn't start crying now. If I did, I would never stop.

Besides, I was tired of crying. It was time to put on my big girl boots and get moving. I had a chance to start over and I was taking it.

I'd cried enough.

I pushed the top of the luggage down and zipped it shut. There. It was done. Everything we owned was inside that bag. The other bag was Hallie's diaper bag. It just held baby stuff; diapers, wipes and snacks for the trip. I had my beat up old purse, a light jean jacket and that was it.

"Are you sure you aren't just doing this so he'll come running after you?"

I shook my head.

"He won't. And since he won't know where I'm going, it doesn't matter. He can't come find me. Right Crys?"

I gave her a hard look and she nodded. I knew she wanted to help. But I didn't need any meddling. It was over. That was it.

"Besides, I don't know if I could forgive him for... her. It was just too soon and I... well, it doesn't matter now."

Crystal nodded. She knew what I was talking about. I'd described the sexy blond at Jagger's place in detail. Down to the fact that her lip was pierced and that she wasn't wearing a bra. He hadn't even waited a whole week to get somebody new in his bed.

But that was none of my business. He'd made that clear. And if he was moving on, I had to move on too. Not to another man. Just... away.

As far away as I could get.

"One last thing?"

"Anything for you toots."

"Can you give me a ride to the bus station?"

She held out her hands, begging me.

"Let me buy you a plane ticket at least."

I shook my head.

"No way. I'm doing this on my own. The honest way. It's all on me."

She titled her head and sighed, looking at me with her big sad eyes. I knew she was holding back tears. Mostly for me, but also because of her elaborate taupe and aqua eye makeup.

"Alright, doll. We'll do it your way."

19
JAGGER

I stood a block away, waiting for the General to leave his house. I'd texted Jenny over and over the past few days but it looked like she'd blocked my number. When I called I didn't even get a voicemail.

Yeah, she'd blocked me alright. Not that I blamed her. I knew how all this looked. I would be pissed too.

Hell, I'd be fucking devastated.

She thought I'd rebounded already. Suze's unkempt appearance didn't help matters. She'd looked like she'd been fooling around. Jenny had no way of knowing that Suze *always* looked like that.

The General had left ten minutes ago. I took a deep breath and jogged to the door. I knew she was going to be pissed. I would be too. But I had to talk to her. To tell her the truth. I just hoped she would listen.

I had spent the last few days imagining how she felt. I knew she was hurt when I'd called it off. Now I was afraid that she thought I'd never been in love with her to begin with.

But that was a lie. The sad truth was, I was *still* in love with her. I had a crazy feeling I always would be.

No matter what she said when she opened the door. Whatever she said, I would stand there and take it. And then I'd tell her who Suze was and maybe, just maybe we could talk about fixing what we'd broken.

What we'd both broken.

But she didn't open the door.

I waited a long time before I realized that either she was hiding from me or she was out. I frowned. The house *felt* empty somehow. It was early for her to be out already with Hallie. It wasn't even zero eight hundred.

Maybe she was already at the playground...

I waited a few more minutes then I left, heading over that way. There were already some moms there, sipping coffee and watching their kids play. I recognized Crystal right away. She wore dark sunglasses and sat alone.

"Hey."

She gave me a look, not bothering to say hello. She did slide over and make room for me on the bench. She sounded disgruntled when she finally spoke.

"Took you long enough."

"What?"

"To notice she was gone."

My blood felt like it had turned to ice.

"What do you mean, gone?"

"Relax, she's not trying to keep your kid from you. She's being mighty fair about it if you ask me."

"What are you talking about?"

She sipped her coffee, staring at me.

"You know, I had you figured all wrong Jagger. I thought you were in it for the long haul. I thought you-"

She pointed her finger right at my chest.

"-were one of the good guys."

I stared at her. I could feel my heart thumping in my chest. I had a terrible, sinking feeling that I had lost Jenny. For good.

"What do you mean she's gone, Crystal? Where did she go?"

"She moved dude. Adios muchacho."

My breath was coming fast now. I felt lightheaded as I tried to figure out what the hell Crystal was saying to me. She'd left? By herself?

"Where is she? Is she safe? Is she alright?"

"No, she's not fucking alright! She was in love with you! You fucked some other girl after she tried to tell you she had your fucking baby! Alone, by the way! She didn't have anyone to help her! Not even me!"

I could just stare at her as she picked up steam.

"You think it was easy being an unwed, teenage mother? Didn't matter that her daddy was the General. None of these bitches wanted to talk to her."

She waved her hand at the other mothers across the playground who were watching us with rapt attention. They gave her a dirty look but didn't look away. How could they? She was practically shouting at me.

"Never mind all the fun stories she got to hear about *you*. Oh yeah, girls talk Jagger. And she got to hear allllll about your conquests, SPD. Also known as Sergeant Panty Dropper."

I flinched. She had a point there. I had been pretty wild back in the day. I could suddenly picture Jenny pregnant, so beautiful and young and afraid.

I was starting to feel like I'd really fucked up. Like I'd been too hard on her. I should have let her talk. I should have listened. I should have been more forgiving.

Each word Crystal said slammed into me like a sledgehammer. She was really on a roll now. She was preaching like she was at church.

"And you- you have a hot little blond lined up not five fucking minutes later! Well done, Jagger! You and your gonads have proved that you are a real bastard! I hope you are fucking proud."

She pointed at my chest again. I flinched but I didn't look away. I deserved this. So I took my medicine. Every last drop.

"It's your fault she's gone. And it's your fault, I lost my best damn friend in the world!"

I was starting to get the picture. Hell, she'd made her point and then some. It *was* my fault. But she wasn't done.

"And now she and that baby are alone, living in some flea trap. If I was a man, Jagger, I'd beat the crap out of you."

I smiled bitterly.

"I'm sure you would."

I closed my eyes.

"Please, Crystal. I need to talk to Jenny. She blocked my number."

She crossed her arms and looked away from me.

"Good!"

"Listen to me Crystal."

"Why should I?"

I sighed, resting my head in my hands.

"The blond is my sister."

"Yeah, right. Jenny told me you are an orphan."

"Not an orphan. My parent's weren't dead. I was unwanted."

She scowled but she was listening at least. I took a deep breath.

"Suzy - the blond - she's my foster sister."

Crystal's overly bright lips opened in surprise.

"No shit?"

I shook my head.

"No shit."

"Where is she, Crystal?"

"Can't tell you. Sworn to secrecy."

She looked away, her arms still crossed. I hadn't earned her forgiveness yet. But I would get her cooperation.

"But she did ask me to give you this."

She pulled something out of her purse and handed it to me. It was an envelope. My name was printed neatly on it.

"What is it?"

She shrugged as I tore it open and read. It was a very polite, very neatly written letter. Jenny had perfect penmanship. But the letter... the letter broke my heart.

Crystal was right. Jenny was more than fair. She told me she was leaving without saying why. It wasn't a Dear John letter. She said nothing about love or breaking up.

It was an offer to co-parent, even if we ended up in different states. She was offering me parental rights, even though she had no real reason to. She told me that I would hear from her lawyer soon and we'd work out something that suited us both.

I closed my eyes.

I'd done this. I knew what it must have cost her emotionally to write that, to even contemplate it. As an unmarried father, I barely had any rights. Seeing Hallie without her permission would have been an uphill battle.

She wasn't asking for child support. She was offering me my child. Giving back what I'd told her she'd stolen. But she hadn't really.

She'd just delayed things a bit.

"Where is she?"

She stared at me, her leg bouncing as she decided whether or not to trust me.

"Please, Crystal."

"Tell me one thing, Jagger. Do you love her?"

"Yes, I fucking love her!"

"Okay, she'll kill me but I believe in happy endings. She's in Charleston. A youth hostel downtown."

She gave me the name of the place and her phone number in case I needed her. I stood up and thanked her. For telling me. And for being a good friend to Jenny. She smiled at me and I turned to go. I had to get a move on if I was going to catch up with my woman.

"Wait, before you go. Just one more thing!"

I was already trying to figure out the quickest way to Charleston. I couldn't take my bike, because we'd be coming back with the baby... Maybe I could hop on a cargo flight to a base nearby...

"What?"

"Did you like her makeover?"

"Her what?"

"The day you came to pick up Hallie. I saw the way you looked at her in that red dress."

I smiled. Suze was right. It *had* been a post break-up makeover.

"I fucking hated it."

Crystal smiled knowingly.

"She looked hot, right?"

I almost laughed.

"Off the charts."

She pulled her arm into her side in a self-congratulatory move.

"I knew it! Okay Jagger, you're forgiven. Go get our girl!"

I gave her a thumbs up as I ran off.

I had to get her back.

I had to.

JENNY

I rocked Hallie back and forth with my foot on the base of the stroller, too busy folding clothes with my hands. I hadn't started at the bar yet, they needed to move the schedule around to make room for me. So for now, I'd found a job at the laundromat, washing and folding.

It was alright, though the heat was starting to get to me. Hallie seemed to like it though, and they didn't mind that I had my baby with me.

In fact, the lady who ran the place had taken a real shine to both of us.

Hallie had some new toys and the owner Ellen had even started knitting her a hat. She said it got cold here in the winter. I had no idea what to expect when I'd come here, so I hung on every word.

It looked like we were going to need winter coats.

One of the reasons I'd chosen Charleston was the schools. Lots of colleges to apply to when I was more settled. Another reason was that Margie knew someone with a job.

But the truth was I was running away. From the constant reminders of what I'd almost had. A man. A stable home for Hallie. From the very good chance that I'd see him around on a regular basis.

With her. The blond.

Or others... probably lots of others.

And the truth was that was pretty much the only reason. I knew I would crumble if I had to keep seeing Jagger around the base. The college stuff had more to do with me trying to talk myself into this being a good idea. Dad hadn't been happy. He'd even tried to give me money, which was out of character to say the least.

But after the mess I'd made of things with Jagger, I was determined to do every single thing on my own. Even pay for a lawyer. I had the appointment tomorrow.

Two hundred and fifty dollars, just to talk.

I shook my head and kept folding. It would take me a week at the laundromat to make that kind of money. But it had to be done.

The only thing about it I hated was the time. It was easy to slip into a trance when you were doing laundry. Your mind tended to wander.

And mine always wandered the same direction.

Jagger, in a t-shirt and jeans. No shoes. The blond behind him. The look on his face when I'd told him the truth.

The look on his face when he told me he didn't want me anymore.

I closed my eyes, trying to block out the pain.

What's done is done. Stop crying about it Jenny. It's over.

Move on.

Except I wasn't going to move on. I didn't want to date anyone else. I wasn't sure I ever would.

I'd compare anyone I met to Jagger.

And they'd come up short.

Their eyes wouldn't be as blue. Their kiss as wild. Their hair as... tousled. I still wondered how he got it to look so damn good. From what I could tell, it was just Jagger. One hundred percent natural.

So I tried to shut him out. And failed.

I started early and worked late, making sure I made every dollar I could. Hoping I would wear myself out enough to sleep without dreaming. Finally, it was time to close up. I smiled down at my sleeping baby.

"Okay kiddo, let's go home."

A slice of bitterness cut through me. Home... haha. That was a joke. We didn't have a proper home.

We didn't belong anywhere.

Or to anyone.

But at least we had each other.

I kissed her head and wheeled us back to the youth hostel to sleep.

20

JAGGER

"w!"

My head bounced against the wall as the plane dipped. Again. I was on the floor, stowed away as a favor by a buddy in the back of a cargo plane. It had been leaving at the right time and heading in the right direction.

I hoped so anyway.

Otherwise, I was going to be shit out of luck.

This flight went to a base a few hours from Charleston. I had a small bag with me and nothing else. I was pretty much going to beg my woman to come back to me.

I knew I was the living embodiment of a country western song.

██████████████████████████████

MY WOMAN DONE LEFT me
  She run far away
  My woman done left me

YEAH. That was me. I put my bag behind my head and held onto the straps that held the massive cases on either side of me. I eyed them, hoping they didn't fall on me. Or that they didn't fall on me and then explode.

This was definitely not regulation.

If they landed on me, *I'd* be the one to get court marshaled.

Even if I got squashed.

I closed my eyes, rubbing my temples. I had to focus. I had to have a plan. What was I going to say to her? Start with the facts. She'd left because she saw Suzey. She thought I'd cheated or at least moved on too quickly.

Which still sounded like cheating to me, considering how recently we were together. More than just together. We'd been madly in love. I sure as shit hoped she hadn't had the same idea... the thought of another man touching her made me sick to my stomach.

So step one was convincing her I hadn't cheated. I had a dog earred photo of Suze and I as gangly teens. One of the few actual photos ever taken of me, before the service and smartphones.

That had to be enough to convince her.

Then I had to make her love me again. If I knew my Jenny, she'd shut me out. Hard. She told me about how she did it with her mother too, not mourning for months and months until it hit her all at once.

She was a tough nut to crack, my girl. I had to make sure I got through to her. I had the photo in one pocket, and a borrowed engagement ring in the other.

Margie hadn't been too happy to see me when I'd stumbled into the bar but I'd made my case anyway. She'd been furious at me for breaking things off with her favorite waitress. I'd taken a verbal licking that was beyond anything my CO's had dished out.

But it was worth it.

She was worth it.

In the end, she'd believed that I wanted what was best for Jenny. That I just might be the man for her. She'd given me a ring and an evil grin as I'd gotten up to leave.

Good luck, Jagger. You'll need it. If you think I'm tough, you have yet to tangle with Jenny.

I grinned. She had that right. And I had a whole lot of tangling to do.

JENNY

"And you want to share custody?"

I nodded, unnerved by the way the lawyer's eyes roamed over me every two seconds. He looked sharp and hungry, like a predator. And he was definitely more interested in my tits than my case.

He leaned back, rubbing his lip.

"You don't need to do this you know."

"What do you mean?"

He shrugged.

"You're not currently in a relationship are you?

I shook my head.

"But if you were to be... sharing custody might create issues."

"I don't understand."

"If you truly give him shared rights than you couldn't move too far away without his explicit agreement. Ideally, both parents live in the same state."

I stared at him. I felt sick thinking about years and years passing, having to live near Jagger. Seeing him but not being able to talk to him. Or touch him.

"What if you started seeing someone in Charleston? He's the employeed party. A Judge could insist you return there so he can support the child."

The lawyer steepled his fingers. I had the oddest feeling that he was talking about himself when he said 'seeing someone in Charleston.' I frowned.

"Derek. His name is Derek."

"Right." He flipped through his notes. "Derek Jagger."

I exhaled, shaking my head.

"I don't want to deprive him of anything. I want Hallie with me for school once she starts, but everything else should be split. If he wants fifty percent, he can have it."

He raised his eyebrows.

"That's unusually generous as a first negotiating point. What if he pushes back? Or wants sole custody?"

"He won't."

"So, the split was amicable?"

I nodded. It had been amicable. If you didn't count me sobbing my eyes out.

Or the blond.

"I want him to be happy with the agreement. We don't need to negotiate."

He held his hands up.

"Alright Ms. Reeds. If you're sure. I'll draw something basic up."

"Thank you."

"We'll get it to you next week."

I shook my head vehemently.

"No. I need it right now."

"That's not how we work. I need to have my staff-"

"Please, I can't afford any extra billing. I gave you everything I have."

He looked at me with a calculating stare. Then his eyes softened. He nodded and I nearly slumped in relief.

Twenty minutes later I stood in the waiting room with the document in hand. The lawyer did ask me out, but I politely declined. I felt a heavy weight lifted as I put the envelope into my purse. He'd send another copy directly to Jagger. It was cleaner that way.

All future arrangements would be scheduled through a third party we would select at a later date. My contact with Jagger would be minimal at best. Maybe I'd be able to bear it someday, but not yet.

I stepped out into the sunshine, willing myself to enjoy the beautiful day. It was green here, and the air was more humid. I touched my hair, which was curling up like crazy and shrugged.

What did it matter what I looked like anyway?

Hallie shook her chubby little arms in the air as I pushed her down the tree-lined street. I headed towards a discount store I'd seen. It was near the shabby neighborhood we'd moved into.

I'd gotten the keys that morning and moved in right away. I had lots of cleaning to do at our new place. It was half of the second story of a two family row house. It was really old, built around the turn of the century. The two-room apartment was nothing fancy, but it was ours.

I almost smiled as we walked through the streets, feeling like I had a plan. Anything was possible. I might even learn to laugh again, if nothing else.

21
JAGGER

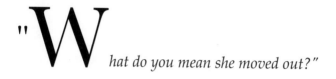"What do you mean she moved out?"

I didn't mean to sound so mean. But I could not believe this was happening. Had Jenny found out I was coming and left the hostel already?

I gripped the edge of the counter, feeling the grit and grime under my hands. This place was a shithole. Maybe she'd found a better place. I hated thinking of her here, all alone.

With our baby.

The front desk attendant was a skinny little twerp. He looked nervous as hell to be facing off against an angry Marine. I didn't blame him.

"Dude, I would totally help you out if I could. But this isn't the sort of place you leave a forwarding address."

I closed my eyes and prayed for patience. Jenny had been gone for days now. I hadn't seen her in over a week. And that last time had been... awful.

I could still see her, looking so beautiful in the rain. Beautiful and fragile and vulnerable. And that was before she saw Suze, guzzling beer in my apartment like she lived there.

I'd hurt Jenny badly, and more than once.

I cursed and walked out of the hostel without a word. I looked around at the seedy cafes and bars in the area. I was not getting anywhere on my own. It was time to call in backup.

I didn't bother with calling any of my war buddies. I went right for the big guns. I called in the girls.

Thankfully, Crystal picked up on the first ring.

"She's not here."

"What?"

"I don't know what to do, Crystal. She's gone."

"Alright take a deep breath. Maybe she found a place already. I haven't heard from her in a few days."

I moaned, covering my face with my hand.

"What about Margie? Would she know?"

"No, I don't think so."

I swallowed.

"The General?"

"Maybe. But if I were you I would use that as a last resort."

I paced up and down the street, trying to imagine how the hell I was going to find her.

"Wait!"

I held my breath, waiting for Crystal to talk.

"I know how to find her! Margie got her a job at a bar, she must know where she works at least."

I thanked Crystal profusely and hung up. I may have promised to babysit her kids. Every weekend. For a year.

I just hoped Jenny would be there to babysit with me.

I said a little prayer and called Margie at the restaurant, hoping she would help me again. Lord knows she'd raked me over the coals already.

"You ask her yet?"

I resisted the urge to roll my eyes. Margie got right to the point. I explained the situation and she gave me a hard time for a few minutes.

"Please Margery. I have this pretty ring of yours and no one to give it to."

She laughed and I felt relief wash through me.

"Sure thing Jagger. It's called Whiskey Wild. I'm just bustin' your nuts."

"I owe you Margie."

"Damn right you do!"

I hung up and looked up the address for Whiskey Wild. It wasn't too far so I walked over there, practicing what I might say. It was mostly 'I'm sorry' and 'please forgive me' with a liberal dose of 'I love you, I love you, I love you.'

Hopefully she'd be more willing to listen than I'd been.

I stared at the bar front, calming my nerves. Thinking of her walking home alone from this place was making me upset. It was in a nicer part of town at least.

Through the window I saw a beautiful girl at the hostess station. I almost didn't recognize her, she looked so sophisticated.

Jenny was in a uniform. A black mini dress, sheer black stockings and heels. I swallowed. I'd never seen her looking like that. She stood straight, her face calm and impersonal as she greeted a group of customers.

She looked like someone else. A rich city girl. The dress was even better than the red outfit Crystal had put her in.

Not better.

Worse.

She was so sexy it hurt to look at her, knowing that she probably hated me. A million guys would kill to go out with her. They wouldn't be so stupid and throw it all away.

I felt my insides clawing at me. I was all twisted up inside. But I had to stay calm and make my case.

I had to woo her back again.

I had to fight for her.

I'd never forgive myself if I didn't try.

I stepped inside the bar and waited until she looked up. She looked at me like I was a phantom of her imagination. For a split-second, I thought she looked glad to see me.

Overjoyed even.

The look on her face made her even more beautiful, if that was possible.

But then something snapped shut in her eyes. Just like that, Jenny was gone. She was someone else. Someone I didn't know. She stood there, looking like a supermodel and gave me an impersonal smile.

The only sign she even knew me was her voice. It was a little shaky as she pulled out a menu and greeted me. The sound tore through me, making me want to hold her and tell her everything would be okay.

But it didn't seem like she wanted to look at me right now, let alone let me touch her.

"Are you alone this evening?"

I nodded brusquely. Did she think I'd brought a fucking date? Or was she just going through the motions?

"And will you be eating or would you like to be seated at the bar?"

My heart broke a little while she did her little hostess spiel. I deserved it though. I'd fucked things up enough.

"Jenny..."

She shook her head, as if warning me not to say her name.

"We have happy hour specials and snacks at the bar. You can get anything off the main menu as well..."

I reached forward, almost touching her arm. She stared at my hand like it was a rattlesnake that might bite her. I dropped my arm and swallowed. I could see she was fighting with herself to stay aloof. That's the last thing I wanted.

I wanted her present, talking to me. I wanted her to scream and cry. I wanted her to yell at me for being an idiot.

I wanted her jealous over Suze. Shouting. Pouring drinks in my face. Hell, I wanted her to smack me.

And then afterwards, I wanted her to forgive me.

"Please Jenny... don't."

JENNY

"Do you- do you want a table then?"

He stared at me, a funny look in his gorgeous blue eyes. He must be upset that I took the baby without telling him. Maybe he hadn't gotten my letter. I had my purse tucked into the hostess station. I'd just give him the envelope and he'd go away.

And I wouldn't have to look at his beautiful face anymore.

"Is there somewhere we can talk?"

I frowned at him, then at the reservation book in front of me. I didn't know what to do. I needed this job and I was new...

I looked around. There were cocktail tables near the hostess stand that were the extent of my section. I had a feeling Margie had put the pressure on them to give me any tables at all, but even if it was pity, I was grateful for them.

Still, he'd come a long way. I could give him the document and let him say his piece. As long as he didn't get me in trouble.

"I have to work, but if it gets slow I can..."

Shit. He was looking at me with those huge eyes of his. He looked tired and upset.

But he wasn't looking at me like a stranger for the first time in weeks. Hope sprang up in my chest. I squashed it down just as fast.

He didn't want me.

He'd said so.

He didn't want me.

"That sounds fine, Jenny. Thanks."

I led him to one of the smaller cocktail tables by the bar and he sat, angling so his back was to the wall. I felt his eyes on me as I took his drink order and walked away. He always did that. Watched me.

It was the protector in him.

It was the thing that was going to make him a great dad.

I had to be grateful for that, at least.

Even if he wasn't perfect. Even if Hallie had lots of his women in her life, I knew he wouldn't expose her to anything bad. Maybe it would be kind of nice. She could call them all 'aunties.'

Then again, I kind of wanted to claw all those imaginary girls' faces off.

I brought over his soda and a menu. Then I stood there, not sure how to bring up the document. I ended up just blurting it out.

"I have something for you."

He smiled at me tenderly and I felt my heart leap. I rushed away before he could see the effect he was having on me. I seated two tables and then grabbed the letter from my bag.

I could feel Jagger watching me the whole damn time. It made me jumpy. I felt hot and cold all over at the same time.

"Here."

I held it out in front of me, forcing myself to meet his eyes. He looked at me, then slowly reached out for the envelope. He opened the folded papers and started to read. I knew I should shut up and just let him read it, but I couldn't. I wrung my hands nervously as I started to babble.

"I saw- a lawyer and he made it real simple. I get her when she's in school and you can split the rest of the time. If you want to. You don't have to."

He looked up from the paper and stared at me.

"Or if you ever lived closer we could share the school week too I guess. I don't know. I didn't... get that far."

I saw his adams apple bob. He needed a shave. He looked like he hadn't slept in days.

I knew the feeling.

"Jenny-"

"I told you I was sorry and I meant it. It just took me a while to trust you with her. But I do now. So- oh shit, I have a table."

I hurried to the front and seated two businessmen. They asked for my section and tried to flirt. I smiled and bit the inside of my lip, knowing this was part of my job.

Besides, douchey guys left the biggest tips.

I went back to my station, watching as Jagger read the document out of the corner of my eye. He pulled something out of his pocket and stared at it. Then he looked at me.

I turned my head so fast I felt like I was going to get whiplash.

The bar was quiet for the next ten minutes. I didn't have an excuse not to go back over to Jagger. I got right to the point. There was no point in dragging this out.

"Are you going to sign it? He charges an arm and a leg so if we need to make adjustments I'd rather we figure it out now so he can just change it once..."

I trailed off, staring into his eyes. He was looking at me like he thought I was beautiful.

He looked like he wanted to kiss me. But that wasn't right. Was it?

"I'll sign it if you want me to. But I have something for you first. Two things actually."

I glanced around to make sure no one was waiting. The two businessmen were slurping back their vodka cocktails pretty quick. I'd have to go over there soon.

"This is the first thing."

He slid a dog earred photo across the table. I picked it up and stared at it. It was a boy... him. A lanky, teenage Jagger. He had his arm slung around a girl with rainbow colored hair. She was pretending to pick her nose, obviously annoyed about having her picture taken.

I looked at him, confused.

"That's Suzy."

I still didn't get it.

"She's my foster sister. The one I told you about. She's blond now. She's the one... you saw that night."

My throat felt tight as I realized what he was saying.

"There isn't anyone else Jenny. There hasn't been in a long time. Not since I met you the first time."

He reached for my hand.

"There couldn't be."

I stared at him, his words sinking in. The gorgeous blond at his place that night... he hadn't slept with her. He hadn't slept with anyone.

He leaned back in his seat and cursed, running his hand through his hair.

"You have a table."

I was back a few minutes later. What he'd told me was nice, but he'd still broken up with me. I wanted to hear what else he had to say.

"What's the second thing?"

"Do you believe me? About Suze?"

He ran his hands through his hair again. It looked slightly less perfect than usual. *Slightly.*

"I hated knowing what you thought. I hated knowing you must hate me."

"I... don't."

His eyes were tormented as he looked up at me.

"I mean, I don't hate you. I believe you."

He smiled at me in relief and it was like the whole room lit up.

The whole world.

I realized why he came all the way here. He wanted me back. I was sure of it now. I wanted to throw myself in his lap and cover him with kisses. But what if I was wrong?

I had to be sure. I couldn't handle another rejection. I couldn't get my hopes up.

"So, what's the other thing?"

He did something I didn't expect then. He got down on one knee. And he took out a ring.

The whole restaurant seemed to get quiet.

"Jennifer Reeds, will you do me the honor of becoming my wife?"

I stared at him, open mouthed. I was in shock. I was ecstatic. Then reality set in. Maybe he was just doing this for our baby. Maybe he just didn't want her to grow up in a broken home.

I wanted to shout yes. But I had to know. So I asked him.

"Are you asking because of Hallie?"

He smiled at me and shook his head.

"I'm asking because I'm in love with you. And I have been since that first night. Jenny, I was going to ask you anyway. The General told me to wait because you were too young."

He smiled at me tenderly.

"But I think you're old enough to make up your own mind about that."

I closed my eyes as the tears started to fall. Then I was nodding my head and crying and laughing at the same time. I tried to say yes but it came out as a whisper. It didn't matter though.

Jagger got the message.

He scooped me up in his arms and twirled me around. I was laughing and crying at the same time. That was a first.

We kissed and kissed and then he sat me down. I wiped off my tears as he held me.

"The ring is just a loan. We can pick out whatever you want when we get back."

I stared at the simple gold band with the diamond chip set in a heart.

"Where did you get it?"

"It's Margie's."

I laughed some more before I realized there was a line forming at the front. I still had a job to do.

"I have to go."

He laughed and nodded. Jagger sat there all night as I went back to work, showing people to their tables. The place filled up and

I brought Jagger dinner. He waited patiently as I finished up my shift.

Well, he was patient until the end. Jagger started to get pissy about a table of young guys who were flirting with me. They were harmless, still in college. But Jagger was watching them like a hawk.

I gave them their check after last call, eager to leave with my fiance. One of the guys grabbed my hand to keep me from leaving. I could almost hear Jagger growl across the section.

"Come out with us tonight, sweetheart. I promise to be a gentleman."

He kissed my hand and I gently pulled it away.

"I'm in love. I think I want to marry you."

I laughed. The kid was drunk and talking nonsense. But that was two marriage proposals in one night.

If that wasn't an ego boost, I don't know what was.

"Thanks but I can't."

"Why not, beautiful?"

"I'm already engaged."

The kid wagged his eyebrows at me.

"What he doesn't know won't hurt him."

I hooked my thumb and gestured over my shoulder to Jagger.

"He'd know."

The kid took one look at Jagger and clammed up. They downed their drinks and left in a hurry. I smiled to myself as I pocketed the enormous tip.

Jagger smiled at me, but he looked a little annoyed. I shook my head and started wiping down the empty tables. It was a little like having an enormous human watchdog.

Sure, I could have survived alone. Even thrived. But I didn't *have* to be alone anymore.

Now, I had backup.

I had Jagger.

22
JAGGER

"**W**hat am I going to do with you, woman? Do men throw themselves at you like that every single day?"

She giggled and shook her head. I looked around Jonny's place. She'd cleaned it top to bottom but it was still a dump. It was safe and clean though, so she'd signed a lease. Didn't matter.

I was going to pay off the landlord tomorrow and take her home.

We'd already checked in on Hallie who was sleeping soundly in a portable crib. It wasn't anything fancy but Jenny had done well for them, finding a way to meet their needs on a severely restricted budget. I'd paid the sitter, a kindly old woman who lived down the block.

I prowled into the room, staring at the twin bed in the living room that served as the couch and the place Jenny slept. It would have to do.

My first instinct was to take her to a fancy hotel and screw her brains out for days. But she said she had to nurse. So I watched as she picked Hallie up and carried her into the living room, which was also her bedroom.

Yeah, it was a dump alright.

She'd found a plastic rocking chair at the discount store and thrown a blanket over it, making it look charming somehow. She sat in it, pulling the top of her tight black dress down. My mouth went dry as her luscious breast came out. She smiled at me flirtatiously and offered her nipple to Hallie.

I'd never been jealous of a child before in my life.

But at that moment...

She winced a bit as Hallie suckled on her. I'd noticed her nipples were sore a lot when we were together, fucking like rabbits most of the time. I'd always been especially careful with her breasts, thinking she was just sensitive. I felt like a fool for not figuring out why.

She was sore because I had been sharing her, that whole time, and just not been smart enough to put two and two together.

Hallie started fussing and before I could offer to take her, Jenny pulled the second cup down. Now her gorgeous body was practically bare to the waist.

I stared in awe as she switched the baby around. Hallie knew the routine apparently because she immediately started drinking from the other breast. Jenny stared down at our daughter, her red hair framing her beautiful face.

It was the most erotic thing I'd seen in my life.

Ten minutes later the baby was clean, fed and ready for bed. I followed Jenny around the tiny apartment, wanting to help. Wanting to touch her.

I was so horny, so desperate for her, I could have cut glass with my hard on. But she wasn't a blow up doll. She'd been on her feet all night. She might be too tired for what I had in mind.

I cleared my throat, leaning in the doorway.

"You must be tired."

She smiled at me over her shoulder, laying Hallie in the crib. She adjusted the blankets and made sure Hallie was in a good position. Then she looked back at me again.

"I'm not."

She closed the door and walked past me to the little bed by the windows.

"But take it easy on my nipples."

I didn't have to be told twice.

JENNY

I ran my hands through his hair, sighing in pleasure. Jagger was raining little tiny kisses all over my face and neck. His fingers gently grazed my chest.

I'd told him to go easy, but this was ridiculous.

Now he was just teasing me.

I tugged on his hair and wrapped one leg around his waist, pulling him towards me. He just shook his head and pulled back. He went back to nibbling on me. I started to wiggle, sure I was going to go insane.

He knelt in front of me and pulled my black heels off. I moaned, it felt so good not to be wearing the painful shoes any longer. I'd bought them for $19.99 at one of those cheap shoe places. They looked good enough for the job but they were cheaply made and bit into my feet in an uncomfortable way. He kissed my foot and I giggled. Then he ran his fingers up and down my stockings.

I shivered and the sensation. He stared up at me, pushing the skirt of my dress up to my hips. I watched in fascination as he scraped his fingers up and down my thighs... behind my knees... and then up the inner thigh... it felt... *ohhhhh.*

"Lay back."

I did as he asked and he kept doing what he was doing. Up and down, finding the sensitive spots, coming close to the top but never touching me exactly where I wanted him to. I sat up and glared at him. He'd taken his shirt off and looked like he was intensely concentrating.

"Jagger..."

"Shhhh... lay back."

He smiled at me.

"Good girls get a reward."

I moaned and slumped back onto the bed again.

He didn't stop for another ten minutes. My hips were rocking by that point. I wanted him so bad I thought I would scream.

"Don't move."

I heard him leave and then riffling around in the kitchen. He was back between my legs. This time he slowly pulled the stockings off me and told me to lift my arms up so he could get my dress off.

He watched me with dark eyes as I lay back again, just in my bra and panties.

"Close your eyes."

I closed them.

"Spread."

I let my thighs part slightly. He tapped the side of my knees sharply.

"Wider!"

I slid them wider until I was in a plie, my feet far apart on the floor.

"Hmmm... good. Very good..."

Something cold touched my ankles and slid up my legs. I gasped as Jagger ran ice up to my inner thighs. I looked at him and he smiled, winking at me as he put a piece in between his lips and held it there.

I gasped as he used his mouth to rub ice down the center of my panties. His fingers were busy too, rubbing my nipples through my bra. I groaned, my hips rocking uselessly. He chuckled and pulled away.

Slowly, ever so slowly, he pulled my panties down. He gently lifted one foot, and then the other, until the panties were gone. Jagger tossed them over his shoulder with a wide grin.

Then he started again.

The icy fingers... the teasing... until finally I felt his breath against my bare pussy. And then the icy tip of his tongue darted up and down the line between my lips. I suppressed a squeal, trying to control myself.

I didn't want to wake the baby right now.

That would be... unfortunate.

For the next half hour I lay there, as he coaxed me to the brink again and again. I'd never been this turned on in my life. I wasn't just turned on.

I was desperate.

"Please Jagger..."

He lifted his head and looked at me. Then slowly he unbuckled his jeans and pulled his cock out. It was hard and huge and perfect, with a shiny bead of precum at the tip. I stared at it hungrily, reaching out to touch him.

He pulled back, wagging his finger at me. Then he slowly dragged the tip of his cock over my pussy lips. I groaned as he held his cock, pulling it away again. I stared as he stroked himself slowly.

"Never leave me again Jenny. Say it."

I stared into his eyes. He was serious. He needed to hear it.

"I'll never leave you again."

"Promise me."

His thumb brushed over my pouty lips and a tremor went through me.

"I- oh God! I promise!"

Then he finally, finally gave me what I wanted.

Him.

23
JAGGER

"No more secrets, Jenny..."

Jenny nodded her head vigorously. I knew she'd keep her promise. Just like I knew she'd agree to anything at that moment.

I inched forward, splitting her tight pussy open. She clenched down on me, trying to pull me in. But I would not be rushed.

As much as I wanted to plunge into her sweetness and never come out again, I needed to lay down the law. Especially now that I had the upper hand.

I wanted to make the most of it.

"Tell me. No more secrets."

I withdrew slightly, until just the very tip of my cock was nestled between her pussy lips. She moaned, rocking her hips.

"Tell me."

"No more secrets."

I slid into her and she let out a squeal. I grinned and pressed my hand over her mouth. I grunted and gave her a few good strokes. Then I pulled almost the whole way out again.

She squirmed underneath me but I was not going to be dissuaded.

"I want another baby."

I reached down and rubbed my thumb over her clit. I could feel her squeezing down on me. I grimaced. She felt so good I was going to lose it.

"Oh...."

"Jenny... I want another baby. Soon. And another one after that."

"What?"

Her eyes were open. She looked at me, coming out of her daze. I rubbed her clit again and she shivered.

"I. Want. Another. Baby."

She looked at me, then down at my cock. I wasn't wearing a condom. She opened her mouth and I slid inside her, pulling out just as fast.

"Oh... yes... yes, okay. Let's... oh God... let's have a baby."

I pushed in again.

"Two. At least two. Maybe three."

"Okay. But... oh God! I want to go back to school."

I nodded.

"Yes. You will. We don't have to rush into the second one. Or the third."

I gave her a long deep stroke.

"I want sex in the morning."

"Hmmm hmmm..."

"No matter how tired we are. Work, school, kids... I want you in my bed every night and underneath me every morning."

"Oh... okay Jagger... hmmfff... yes, yes, yes!"

I drove into her again.

"On top of me too."

"Uhhhh..."

I grinned at the woman beneath me. My woman. She was incoherent, her head tossing back and forth on the pillow.

I decided to throw something fun in for good measure.

"And every Sunday..."

"Hmmfff..."

I thrust into her again.

"I want- to- oh fuck- just have-"

I was having trouble talking at this point too.

"Oral!"

She was shaking her head back and forth as I fucked her senseless. I reached between us to stroke her clit. This time I stroked it rapidly, knowing she would come pretty much on command at this point.

"Say yes Jenny."

"Yeh-ehsssss!"

I slammed my hand over her mouth, gently of course. She squealed into my palm as I worked my finger on her clit and my cock in her pussy in perfect tandem. She was shaking and shimmering all over my shaft.

I leaned down and kissed the sensitive part of her neck for good measure. That's when I felt her flood me, her body soaking my cock in her juices.

And then she screamed.

I tried to contain the noise. I tried. But it was too loud.

It woke Hallie up.

I groaned as she stared at me, still shaking as she creamed all over my cock. I was so close. I didn't want to stop.

"I- have to- oh God!"

"Shhh... it's okay. I'll get her."

I pulled out, wincing at the sudden loss of heat and sensation. I yanked my pants on as Jenny rolled back into the bed and watched me. She was still shaking as I walked into the other room to get Hallie.

I left the light on, staring down into the crib. Hallie stopped crying, staring up at me in wonder. It was like looking into a mirror, except she was a whole hell of a lot prettier than I was.

She took after her mama like that.

But the coloring... the shape of her eyes and chin. That was all me. The lips and sweet little nose were Jenny's. The stubborn little chin too.

I smiled tenderly and lifted her up, cradling her against my chest. She made a soft gurgling sound and I felt my heart melt with love. Every damn thing about her was perfect.

Jenny came in, a thin sheet wrapped around her. She looked so beautiful I felt like I might explode with all the emotions welling up inside me. I looked at my daughter, and back at my bride-to-be.

I was glad it was dark so Jenny didn't see the tears welling up in my eyes.

"Is she wet?"

I nodded. She reached for her but I shook my head.

"You lie down. I'll do it."

She crossed her arms and looked at me with a raised eyebrow.

"Do you even know how to change a diaper?"

"Yes, I do. Foster care, remember?"

I gave her a look.

"Get in that bed woman. I'm not done with you yet."

JENNY

I smiled up at Jagger, grabbing another ice chip from the cup on the floor. His knees were spread and I was between them, slowly licking and sucking on his heavy balls.

His heavy, yummy, extremely *full* balls.

He grimaced as I rolled the ice in my mouth against his sac.

"Fuck... Jenny... please..."

"It's after midnight Jagger. That makes it Sunday."

He groaned and let his head fall back as I slid my fingertips over his shaft, teasing the tip.

"You made the rules."

"I- oh God- I take it back. Today is... an exception."

I brushed my lips over the tip of his cock. I was no expert in blow jobs, but I seemed to be doing something right. Jagger had never looked quite this... out of control to me.

He was desperate to come. To have more pressure. To have me.

I knew how he felt.

"Are you *sure* you want me to stop?"

I pulled the tip of his cock into my mouth and swirled my chilled tongue over it, my hand caressing his balls. His hips jerked and I noticed his leg was starting to shake. He shook his head vehemently as I stopped and titled my head.

"No- don't stop. Please-"

I grinned and eased my lips over his cock head, using my tongue to stroke him as I started to bob my head up and down. I used my hands to make up for the lack of depth- no way I was getting that monster all the way inside my mouth!

He grunted as I worked him, staring at me like I was giving him the best head he'd gotten in his life. I took him as deep as I could, flattening my tongue against the underside of his cock. Then I slid to the top, fluttering my tongue against his ridge.

I leaned back and blew on him. He flinched, watching breathlessly as I got another ice chip. I held it in my mouth, sliding my open lips up and down his cock without taking it inside my mouth. I pulled the tip in and sucked on it, before going back to his balls.

He cursed and then next thing I knew I was on all fours, facing the other way. I could see him in the reflection of the dresser mirror, desperately guiding his raging hard on to my pussy.

I gasped as he drove into me. He wasn't gentle. He reached forward to grip my hair, twisting it into a ponytail and pulling my head up so that my back arched. Our eyes met in the mirror. Then he looked down, watching as his cock slid in and out of my body.

Watching *him* watch *us* was... it was the most erotic thing I'd seen in my life.

His hands flexed on my hips and he groaned.

"I'm not going to last Jenny... Fuck, I'm sorry I can't wait."

Considering how long we'd been fucking around, I was surprised he hadn't exploded in my mouth. But I was too busy coming to do anything more than moan.

I felt him expanding, his bare cock pressing deep into my sensitive walls. He grunted like an animal as his tempo increased. I was still coming, still feeling the electricity that passed between us when we came together.

Only this time it was different.

Because he wasn't wearing a rubber.

It felt like... it felt like it had that morning. That morning when we'd conceived Hallie.

I bit my lip to keep from screaming as I felt the first rope of come fill me. It did something to me. Made my orgasm more intense.

Much, much more intense.

Jagger started mumbling nonsense words as he rammed into me, his cock pulsing out his seed. He held my hips and pushed my head down so he could get all the way inside me. He'd never been deeper.

He groaned as his cock expanded, throbbing intensely as thick jets of come shot from his cock. He couldn't be any farther inside me. He was deliberately trying to seed me.

I smiled dazedly as my body clamped down on him with all I had.

I had a sudden feeling that it had worked.

Either way, I knew I'd never forget this night.

It was ten minutes later before we spoke again. Both of us were quiet, relaxed as we cleaned up and slid into the twin bed, snuggled close together. I realized that we would be doing this for the rest of our lives, though hopefully in a bigger bed. This was perfect though, just having him with me made everything perfect.

I smiled, grazing his chest with my fingertips.

"I have a request too."

"What's that, sweetheart?"

"I want a mirror in the bedroom."

He let out a laugh and kissed my temple, pulling me even closer against him.

"Yes, sweetheart. We can have a mirror."

He kissed me deeply and I felt his cock growing between us. He leaned forward and whispered in my ear.

"And here I thought you were going to ask for an ice machine."

"Yes, sir. This model has the highest safety rating of all SUV's in its class."

I nodded. I had done the research early that morning. I was going to buy it. I just wanted to make sure.

Kick the tires and what not.

"What color are you thinking about?"

"What colors can I drive out of here today?"

The salesman grinned, realizing he'd made a sale. About an hour later, I was walking through the sales lot with a set of keys.

He'd driven a hard bargain at first. And then he'd found out I was military. Suddenly, the price was a lot more reasonable.

I stopped at a big box store for a car seat and a case of water. I got diapers, baby wipes and a few things I thought Jenny might need.

And whipped cream.

A whole case of whipped cream.

If she'd liked the ice, I had a feeling she was going to love being my dessert even better.

And I knew I would like being dessert for *her*.

I adjusted my cock as I got into the car. Just thinking about how she'd looked kneeling between my thighs was making me hard again. Never mind all the wicked things she'd done with her mouth...

I drove back to her soon to be ex-apartment and waved. Jenny was on the stoop, holding Hallie on her lap. I felt pride swell up at the sight of them.

Those two beautiful girls were mine.

"All set?"

She nodded.

"We should take the travel crib and everything. Seems a shame to leave it behind."

I smiled.

"That's why I bought big blue."

Her eyes were wide as she stared at the sky blue SUV.

"You bought it?"

I nodded.

"I want my ladies riding home in style and comfort. Airbags and what not."

"But- Jagger- you don't need to spend that kind of money on us."

"Hush darlin'. That's exactly what I need to spend money on. I'm a family man now."

I pulled her close and grinned at the adorable blush on her face.

"Besides, I can afford it."

She looked at me.

"You can?"

"Yes sweetheart. They pay pilots pretty well. And it's kind of hard to spend a lot overseas."

Her pretty pink lips opened.

"Oh."

Then she shook her head.

"But I still want to work."

"Of course, sweetheart. If you want to. *After* you finish college."

Now she was smiling, her eyes shining bright.

"You didn't forget."

"My word is my bond, Jenny. And I meant what I said about Sundays."

She smiled at me, hoisting Hallie onto her hip.

"You better."

I grinned and packed the car with her stuff. There wasn't much so it didn't take too long. I settled Hallie in her car seat and adjusted the straps. I was going to drive slowwwww.

I had precious cargo aboard.

It took almost six hours to get home. I knew I could have made the trip in half the time on my motorcycle but I didn't care. We talked the whole time, except when Jenny dozed off.

Then I talked to Hallie.

She watched me driving, her eyes bright blue in the rearview mirror. I loved the way she smiled at me. I could have sworn she laughed a few times too.

Oh yeah, she was gonna be a daddy's girl alright.

It was dark when I pulled up in front of my place and started unloading. I'd told Jenny the two of them were staying with me, starting tonight. I was done having her away from me, ever again.

Talking Jenny into moving in was the easy part.

I knew tomorrow was going to be the hard part.

Tomorrow I had to face the General.

JENNY

I woke up smiling in Jagger's big, strong arms. It was the second morning in a row and the reality was starting to set in. He loved me. I loved him. We were going to get married.

It was hard to believe that just a few days ago I'd felt so alone. And now I was... not.

I felt safe and warm, snuggling in a little further. Hallie was still quiet in the room next door. Everything felt perfect. Jagger always made me feel desired but it was more than that.

He made me feel cherished.

I giggled as he started making snuffling noises in my neck, like he was an animal rooting around for something. His hands slid over me from behind, smoothing over my bare skin. Behind me, his erection pressed into my backside in a particularly naughty way.

"Jagger!"

"We have a deal, remember? You promised me morning sex."

I nodded, my body already responding to his closeness. "Yes, but we have to be quick.

And quiet." Then I arched my back, rubbing my bottom against his length.

He moaned and nipped my shoulder. I felt him position himself behind me. I was already wet as he rubbed his cock against me. We lay there, spooning as he slowly pressed his shaft inside me.

Jagger started to fuck me slowly, and very, very quietly.

Something about being quiet, about the small, concentrated thrusts, made it even naughtier than regular sex.

This was sneaky don't-wake-the-kids sex.

And I liked it.

I came quickly, with a little help from Jagger's nimble finger. He whispered something about a reach around and I stifled a hysterical giggle. It wasn't long before he was coming too.

I could feel his seed inside me as I lay there, watching him get dressed. His essence. He took one look at me and whistled.

"You look good with my cream pie."

I threw a pillow at him but didn't move. I wanted another baby with him. Laying here for a while before cleaning up would help move that along.

"How do I look?"

I nodded my approval and he pressed a quick kiss on my lips.

"We can go ring shopping later. First I need to go and talk to your father."

I sat up in alarm.

"I should be there too."

He shook his head, looking a little grim. I leaned slowly back down again.

"I think I need to do this alone. It might not be pretty."

I stared at him, thinking that was a gross understatement.

I wished him luck, praying that my father didn't shoot him.

"Jagger, if he pulls out his gun, hit the ground."

He looked at me and nodded.

I had the craziest feeling I was sending my man off to war.

25

JAGGER

"**I**f you are looking for Jenny, she's gone.

Thanks to you."

I stared at the General, my hat in my hand. This time I'd worn my entire dress uniform. I was here to prove myself.

And to grovel.

Oh yeah, it was a good thing I had strong knees. There would be lots of begging done today. Lots and lots of it.

"I'm here to see you, General Reeds. May I come in?"

He just stared at me.

"What do you want?"

"I'm here to discuss Jenny's future. And Hallie's too, of course."

He stared at me. I was still outside. I was not sure he was going to let me in until I told him the truth.

"Is that what your problem was? That she has a kid?"

"No. My problem was that it was *my* kid. And she didn't tell me until a few weeks ago. But I was wrong to hold it against her, sir. I'd like to discuss our future as a family."

His eyes got wide. He took a step forward. I could see his fist clench.

Then he stepped to the side and made room for me to come in.

I took a deep breath as I walked into the lion's den.

He sat in an easy chair and reached for a drink. He looked me up and down. Once again, he didn't ask me to sit.

"What do you want then?"

"I am here to ask for your daughter's hand in marriage."

He snorted.

"It's a bit late for that. You should have kept your damn fly shut- what is it now? Two years ago?"

I stared him right in the eye.

"Just about."

"You have a lot of nerve coming in here and asking me that, when you defiled my teenage daughter. She was a good girl! Until-"

"Until her mother died. I know Jenny, sir. I know who and what she is. And I love her."

He looked at me in surprise.

"She was wild the night I met her. Drinking but not drunk. By herself. Asking for trouble. I think I fell in love with her in the first five minutes."

He narrowed his eyes at me.

"I told myself that if she didn't like me, I'd just see her home. But she did like me. It was one of those things. Fate maybe."

I lifted my chin.

"But I don't regret one second of it. I just wish I'd known how to find her. I wish I'd know about everything she faced without me. So I could have done this two years ago."

He took a sip of his drink and stood.

"I'll give you my answer. After."

"After what?"

"After this."

The General was taking off his belt. For a moment, I wondered if he was going to take a piss on me, and then I saw the way he was holding the belt.

Jenny's father was going to whoop me.

Literally.

He took a swing at me with the belt and I jumped out of the way. He swung it again and it nearly hit my leg. I turned and jumped again, feeling like I was in a cartoon. One of those ones about the cat and the mouse. Or the one where one cowboy shoots at the other one's feet while he dances.

I felt like an idiot but I didn't have a choice. I had to evade until he lost steam. He cursed and tossed the belt away, then came at me, swinging his fists. The General was older, but he was not out of shape.

Not by a long shot.

It didn't matter that I could have theoretically taken him. The reality was that I didn't stand a chance in hell. This wasn't a fair fight.

In fact, it wasn't a fight at all. It was a beat-down. An asswhooping of the highest degree. And if I had to take it to get the old man to agree to let me marry his daughter, I would.

I couldn't hit Jenny's father. She'd never forgive me. Besides, he outranked me by a hundred miles. And I was still waiting for him to agree to the wedding, never mind have his daughter living in sin with me until then.

So I had to just stand there and take it.

I backed away until I ran out of rug. I was in the corner, pressed up against the wall. He reached out and grabbed my collar, twisting it. He lifted me up until I was on my toes. I was a big guy. The General must have been insanely strong when he was my age, if he could lift me up even a few inches now.

I held my hands up in surrender, trying to use a placating tone of voice.

"Please General, let's just talk this out. I'm not going to fight you."

"No, you're not. You're just going to stand there and bleed. If you're lucky, I'll let you live for what you did to my little girl."

"Enough!"

We turned in unison to see Jenny standing in the open doorway.

"Put him down, Daddy."

JENNY

My father was an idiot. My fiance was an idiot. Basically, I was surrounded by idiots.

Sweet, handsome idiots.

I glared at them, seated on opposite sides of the long sofa. Daddy glared at Jagger. Jagger looked at my dad with more than a trace of nervousness. I'd never seem Jagger afraid of anything.

Until now.

I almost laughed at how ridiculous they looked. Like two cowed dogs, snapping at fireflies. But I was too annoyed to laugh.

"How am I supposed to marry him if he's all bruised up, Daddy?"

"He took off on you and Hallie! He's a dead beat!"

I sighed and spoke slowly as if my father was a small child and not a General in the United States Armed Forces.

"Daddy. It was an accident. It wasn't his fault he wasn't around. He didn't know."

He scowled and looked away.

"You honestly want to marry this cretin?"

I glanced at Jagger, who was starting at his hands with a guilty look on his face. He looked like a little boy, who'd been caught with his hand in the cookie jar. Which was pretty much exactly what had happened.

Except *I* was the cookie.

And he'd done a lot more than steal a cookie. He'd gotten the cookie pregnant. I smiled.

"Yes, Daddy. He's a good man and I love him."

Jagger looked at me with a dawning smile.

"Even if his hair is a little *too* perfect."

Jagger's smile grew even larger. He gave me a smug, but endearing look. I knew he was fighting the urge to run his hands through his hair.

Damn him, it wasn't fair that he had a better 'do than me.

Even Crystal thought his hair was amazing, and that was saying something. She'd asked me a while back to look through his medicine cabinets to see what products he used, but I'd declined. Maybe now that we were getting married though, he'd let me in on his grooming secrets.

"We're getting married, Daddy. And he's going to be a good father to Hallie. And any other babies that come along."

"More babies?"

He roared and shot to his feet. I crossed my arms and stared at him until he slowly sat down again. It took a minute, but I wasn't going to back down.

"Would that really be a bad thing, Daddy? Jagger and I almost lost each other. But we got a second chance. And we got Hallie. Wouldn't you like another little kid around?"

He nodded sheepishly.

"That girl is the light of my life. Other than you."

I smiled and sat on the couch between them, grasping each of their hands.

"Come on, now. Play nice. After all, y'all are about to be related."

They stared at each other with a little bit of shock. I laughed. I guess they hadn't really thought all that through.

"Stand up now."

They stood up and faced each other.

"Shake hands."

My father grumbled a bit. "You aren't living under his roof until you're wed." I smiled to myself. I had a feeling he was going to make one last stand.

Jagger opened his mouth to argue but I nodded.

"Alright Daddy, you win. Now shake."

Jagger held his hand out and slowly, very slowly, the General shook it. And shook it. I watched as they tried to crush each other's hands.

I swatted them apart and took Jagger's arm.

"He's going to walk me over to Crystal's to get Hallie. Then I'll be back. You can bring my stuff by later, right Jagger?"

He nodded and we walked out, leaving my father staring after us with a clearly suspicious look on his face. The second we were out the door Jagger swept me into his arms and kissed me. I kissed him back before smacking his shoulder.

Hard.

"You are an idiot. I could have handled him without you."

Jagger stared at me, clearly preoccupied.

"Jenny... you can't move back in here. How are we ever going to be alone?"

I sighed. I knew my father. Now that he knew Jagger was Hallie's daddy, he was going to make him suffer.

"We aren't. Not until the wedding."

He swallowed, looking tragic.

"How long will that take to set up?"

I shrugged, taking his arm as we walked towards Crysal's house.

"I'm not sure. I'm thinking at least a month or two."

"A month?"

I nodded, thinking to myself I could probably get something small together in two weeks. I'd tell him soon. But it was too much fun to watch him stew.

"What's wrong Jagger? What's the big deal?"

He looked at me, his face strained and miserable.

"Jenny, that's too long. *That's four Sundays!"*

2 6
JAGGER

Five days. Five days since I'd been alone with my fiance. The mother of my child. The love of my life.

Five days and my balls were full to bursting.

Oh, I'd seen her. We'd gone out to dinner and taken walks with Hallie. The General even let me come in and sit in the living room with the baby.

But he wasn't letting his eye off his daughter until the wedding. A few stolen kisses. That was it.

I was irritable. Unable to sleep. Crankier than a drunk in church.

Speaking of church... I had pushed and pushed until Hallie moved the wedding date up to next weekend. A whole 'nother seven days away.

I wasn't going to make it. I'd explode in a burst of sweat and sperm first. Seeing her, being around her and not being able to touch her... well, it was fucking torture.

But tonight, *tonight* that was going to stop.

Tonight, I was getting my bride alone. Just for an hour or so. And I was going to use every Goddamn *second* of it.

My opportunity would come after the surprise party we'd put together for her. Well, not me. Margie and Crystal. Hell, even the General was in on it. He'd agreed to baby sit Hallie for the second half, after the cake. If people stayed and got rowdy.

That was the only window of opportunity to get my hands on my girl.

I smiled as she opened the door, having no idea the day I had in store for her. She was dressed in jeans, her thickest pair. Sturdy little boots on her feet. A pretty pink top peeked out from underneath her close fitting denim jacket.

"Hello, sweetheart."

'Hi Jagger."

She smiled at me shyly and walked to the bike, my eyes unable to look away from her sweet little ass. She loved riding with me now. And until she was pregnant again, I planned to take her out whenever I could.

I frowned, thinking I needed to take her shopping for proper gear. She'd need leathers to ride with me in the future. Especially, if we were going farther than ten minutes off base. But this was a damn sight better than riding in a sundress.

Still, the future Mrs. Jagger did look mighty fine in those jeans.

She smiled at me and put her helmet on. I made sure it was locked in and pressed a small kiss on her lips. I had a feeling the General was watching out the front window so I didn't want to push my luck.

I was still afraid he might shoot me.

"Where to?"

I put my helmet on and grinned at her.

"I thought we'd just ride for a little bit."

"Okay."

She looked so sweet and happy as she watched me climb on. Soon her arms and legs were wrapped around me, holding me tight. It felt good.

So good, that I started to get hard.

I quickly turned the engine over and took off, trying to ignore the raging wood in my pants. She always did this to me. I would bet good money that she always would.

I pictured us playing a game of grab ass as we ran around our kitchen at eighty years old.

I couldn't keep the big grin off my face as we peeled off into the sunset.

JENNY

"What are we doing here?"

Jagger shrugged, helping me off the bike. We'd just rode around for a while, always sticking close to base. Then he pulled into the juke joint where I used to work.

"I'm a little hungry. Thought you might be too."

I handed him my helmet and he gave me a small smile as he took my hand, kissing the back of it. Then he led me into the bar. I squinted in the darkness.

Was there a power outage or something?

"SURPRISE!"

I almost jumped into the air as the lights came on. Gary and Margie were there, and the other staff I'd become friendly with. So were Crystal and her husband, Dave. Even the General was there, holding Hallie in his arms.

He wasn't smiling. But he wasn't frowning either.

I turned to Jagger, staring up into his eyes. "What... is this?"

"It's an engagement party, sweetheart."

I looked up at him and felt all the love in my heart swelling up and spilling over.

"You did this?"

He shook his head. He gestured to Crystal and Margie, who stood there with identical smiles on their faces. The sneaky bitches.

God, I loved them.

"They did."

I was trying not to cry as the girls enveloped me. They swarmed me, hugging and kissing me again and again.

Margie offered me a sparkly fizzy looking drink and I shook my head. I'd have to pump and dump. But Crystal took it and pressed it into my hand.

"You better drink this. You *do* realize your name is going to be Jenny Jagger, right?"

I laughed. I did know that. It *was* kind of hilarious.

"Maybe we could get Derek to agree to take Reeds instead."

"Or hyphenate!"

We started laughing so hard we nearly bent over. The place was closed until six for our private party so we made the most of it. When the doors opened a few hours later, the party didn't stop.

287

Dad had eaten ribs with the rest of us. He'd even shared a beer with Jagger. I could see him melting a bit towards my future husband and hid a smile.

The General scooped Hallie out of Margie's arms and walked to the door. He kissed my cheeks and told me to have fun. Then he grumbled something about having to change Hallie's diaper.

I laughed, Margie's special fizzy drinks making me feel a little light-headed. She'd told me it was sparkling water, grapefruit juice and tequila.

Whatever it was, it was delicious.

I took another glass from Margie and sipped it, squealing as Jagger pulled me into his lap. He nuzzled my ear and I got tingly all over. His hands were warm on my hips as he whispered into my ear.

"Let's get out of here."

"Where?"

"My place. You dad won't be expecting you back for an hour or two at least..."

I nodded and we headed outside to his bike. He hadn't had more than one beer and that was a few hours ago. I knew he was fine to ride. He was very careful with safety stuff, and I was grateful for it.

He kissed me deeply before getting on the bike. He was already hard. It had been a whole week since we made love that morning at his place. I knew this was going to be intense.

I felt like I was flying as we rode the dusty road back to base. My fingertips slid over Jagger's stomach, brushing his swollen cock. It was huge and so ready. I couldn't hear him over the wind but I could have sworn he said something.

Either way, the bike picked up speed.

A lot of speed.

We pulled up to the gate and stopped. They didn't wave us through, which was odd. Instead they asked for Jagger's ID.

"Sergeant Jagger?"

Jagger nodded, giving me a look over his shoulder.

"Come with me please."

"Uh... I'm kind of busy, guys."

"This is a direct order. Report to the flight school immediately. Alone."

"On whose orders? It's Saturday night!"

The soldier at the gate shook his head.

"It's not a request Sergeant."

I hid a smile. I knew this was my father's doing. This had the General written all over it.

"I have to drop my fiance off first."

"You have five minutes, Sergeant. You're being timed."

He cursed and took me home. He pulled me against him as soon as I was off the bike, kissing me passionately.

Then he whispered in my ear.

"I'm going to kill your father."

I laughed.

"Please, no actual violence. I'm sure you can find some other way to get even with him."

He brushed his fingers over my face and kissed me.

"I'm going to leave my bike here."

I nodded.

"Good idea."

"Maybe I can sneak in later. Leave your bedroom window open for me?"

I shook my head.

"Not a chance."

He cursed again and handed me his helmet. Then he kissed me quick and took off at a jog. I knew he'd just make that five-minute deadline.

My dad was smiling ear to ear as he opened the front door and waved at Jagger's back. I laughed. It was weird, but I hadn't seen my dad so happy in years.

He really enjoyed torturing Jagger. It was like it had given him a new purpose in life. I had a feeling this was just the beginning.

I shrugged. Hey, whatever worked.

27
JAGGER

This was it. Today was the day. I was getting married.

Every day since I met Jenny had been leading up to this moment. Hell, every day since I was born. Every day since Jenny was born too.

And our darling angel of course.

Objectively, I knew the bride and groom were well matched. We loved and respected each other. We had no secrets or hidden agendas. Not anymore.

It was true love.

We were getting hitched at a restaurant in town, the fancy one I'd taken Jenny to for our first 'real date.' The one with the beautiful garden out back.

That was where it was going to happen. Soon. I was ready and waiting. I was just waiting on the bride.

But not one Goddamn other thing about this wedding had been normal so far.

I shook my head. No bachelor party for me. The General's idea of a stag party was getting the groom shit faced and making him run laps.

Lots and lots of laps.

The guys from the flight school had ambushed me last Saturday night, tied me up and made me do shots. Then they made me run laps and do pushups. The General had even stopped by late night to grin at me.

Right before I puked.

Even Lefoy had been there cheering me on, the shitburger.

The whole week leading up to the wedding had been full of unexpected staff meetings and inspections. For someone who was a pilot instructor and not a grunt, I was getting my ass handed to me on a daily basis. But it was worth it. It was all worth it.

Because today I was getting marrying Jenny Reeds. That meant that I was getting the woman of my dreams. It also meant the wedding night.

I was finally going to get my hands on my beautiful bride. All over her. All night.

For the rest of our lives.

It was a good thing too because I was ready to take off like a Goddamn rocket. Being around Jenny, knowing she loved me and wanted me, and not having her...

It was hell, plain and simple.

But tonight would be heaven. If I made it that far. I kept thinking of ways I could sneak her out of here during the party. Maybe right after the ceremony.

I tugged on my tie, looking around the room. It would be hard as fuck to sneak out though. And Jenny might not want to leave her guests. People had come a long ass way to see us get married. A lot of guys I'd served with were there too, including K-Dawg and company.

Even Joss had sent a wedding gift.

The iceman had melted. I looked at the card and laughed to myself. *Welcome to the Club, you nutjob.* He had that right. I was crazy.

Crazy in love.

I waved to Margie where she sat holding Hallie, bouncing the sweet baby up and down on her thigh. Gary was there too, along with most of the staff. The other guys who taught at the flight school were there too.

And Suze was standing beside me, looking almost mainstream in a soft pink dress. She'd even taken out some of her piercings for this. I smiled at her and she winked.

Jenny had offered to make her a bridesmaid but Suze had looked so horrified that I'd jumped in. I offered to make her best man instead. That was an offer she couldn't refuse.

Thankfully, Jenny and Suze hit it off the second time they met. Now they were thick as thieves. Lord help me if I ever pissed either one of them off because the other one would kill me.

The crowd got quiet and music started to play.

I turned towards the aisle and stood up straight and proud.

It was happening.

It was time.

My heart was racing as I waited. Jenny stepped onto the white aisle runner holding the General's arm and time stopped. She looked beyond perfect in a simple white strapless dress that flowed out behind her.

Her creamy skin gleamed on her exposed chest and shoulders. Her wavy red hair was half up and half down, curled into loose ringlets that made her look like a fairy princess. She held white roses in her clasped hands.

But it was the look in her beautiful eyes that knocked the wind out of me.

She was staring at me with all the love in the world in her eyes.

I stood up even straighter and loved her right back.

JENNY

I took a deep breath and took the first step. Jagger looked a little shell shocked as I walked down the aisle towards him. His eyes were appreciative as he took me in.

Very, *very* appreciative.

I had a feeling it was going to be a long wedding night. A break the headboards and up to see the dawn kind of wedding night. I hoped so anyway.

I stared into his eyes, loving how he looked in his uniform. He even had a white rose in his lapel. His famously tousled hair was slicked down for once.

I couldn't wait to run my fingers through it and mess it up.

We got to the end of the aisle. My father kissed my cheek before I placed my hand in Jagger's. He squeezed it, and stared at me. I tried to smile but he was so serious that I could only stare back at him, getting lost in his stormy blue eyes.

The Judge began the ceremony. It was short and sweet, with no religious undertones. As much as I might have wanted a church wedding, it just wasn't possible with

Jagger's timeline. He'd wanted to get married two weeks ago.

My man had been very insistent about us not waiting too long.

He'd even suggested we fly to Vegas or make a quick stop at the courthouse. He'd wanted to get married the moment the General gave his approval. But I put my foot down. I wanted a proper wedding.

This was our compromise.

And what a wonderful compromise it turned out to be.

A tiny, beautiful, intimate wedding.

It was perfect.

It seemed like just minutes before we were saying our vows. I stared into Jagger's eyes as I said mine. Then it was Jagger's turn. He said his vows and I swear, I felt like there was an invisible chain linking us together.

A chain made of something light and strong and unbreakable.

"You may kiss the bride."

Jagger stared into my eyes for a heartbeat before his lips came crashing down on mine. He kissed me so long that the crowd started to titter. Then Hallie let out a wail and everyone laughed. Even Jagger laughed, picking me up to twirl me around.

That was it.

We were married.

I was Mrs. Jenny Louise Jagger.

The party was a whirlwind of champagne and delicious food and congratulations. When it came time for the first dance I told Jagger I was sorry for everything the General had put him through this week. I was just finding out about half of it from his buddies.

Jagger told me to look at my father.

I stifled a laugh as Jagger spun me around the dance floor so I could get a good look.

He'd gotten his revenge alright.

The General was surrounded by single older women. A few employees from the base, but also some ladies I'd never seen before. Jagger had invited them. He whispered into my ear and I got chills.

"Revenge is sweet."

My husband was diabolical alright. I grinned as he tugged me into the bushes and messed up my hair before we got pulled back to the party again. Crystal whisked me away to fix it before she let anyone see me.

The party was still going strong close to midnight when Jagger whispered to me to meet him out front. His motorcycle had been covered with cans and streamers. He just shook his head and told me to climb on. I tucked my wedding dress up and held up the bouquet

We were only riding it for a block.

I heard everyone rush out and I tossed my bouquet. One of the women leaning on my father's arm caught it and smirked up at him. Everyone cheered as we rode away, to the hotel Jagger had booked for the night. It was the only hotel in town and he'd booked the honeymoon suite.

Tomorrow we left for the real honeymoon.

Two weeks in Hawaii.

A wedding gift from the General.

Of course, we were bringing Hallie with us. So tonight was the only night we'd truly be alone. And I had a feeling Jagger was going to make the most of it.

We checked in and he practically ran up the stairs to our room. I was on the verge of cracking up as he fumbled with the room keys. We walked inside and I smiled. The bed was covered in rose petals. There was champagne in an ice bucket with two glasses on a table by the window.

Then I saw it.

There was an open box in the middle of the room.

"Is that... a wedding gift?"

He shook his head.

"No love. That's a snack. For me. I've been saving it since Charleston."

He grinned at me in a way that sent shivers down my spine.

"And you can have some too, if you're a good girl."

I pulled back the cardboard flaps and looked inside. It was... an entire case of whipped cream. I looked at my husband and back at the box.

"Aren't you too full to have all this sweet stuff?"

He started stripping and shook his head, his eyes never leaving mine. He hadn't eaten much at the wedding, come to think of it.

"Not even close love. Now, strip. Unless you want to get that pretty dress of yours all sticky."

He grinned.

"The bottom part, anyway."

I squealed and ran away. He caught me, spinning me to face him. He kissed me hungrily, grinding his cock into me.

"Tonight I'm having dessert before the main course."

Five minutes later I found myself naked on the bed watching as Jagger gave me a whipped cream bikini.

He took his time applying it, then sat back to survey his handiwork. He pursed his lips, then leaned over me and started licking. I gasped as his tongue slid all over my breasts. He gobbled up every last bit of whipped cream, working his tongue over my nipples way after they were already clean.

He smiled at me before sliding his way down my body to nestle between my thighs. He nipped the sensitive skin on my inner thigh before getting to work. He started by slowly sliding his tongue up and down my pussy lips. I sighed in pleasure, wiggling a bit. I was impatient to have him inside me.

But I wanted to taste him first.

He licked my pussy clean, then honed in on my clit. He pulled it into his mouth and flicked his tongue against it rapidly. I shot off

302

the bed, my hips shaking as I came instantaneously.

"Oh oh oh OH!"

He was grinning by the time he sat up, wiping the sticky sweetness off his face.

I reached for the can of whipped cream but he snatched it away.

"Yours is going to have to be a midnight snack, love. I'm not going to make it five seconds."

I pouted as he tossed the whipped cream across the room.

"But I'm happy to let you have dessert for breakfast. After all..."

I smiled at him as he pushed his pants down.

"Tomorrow *is* Sunday."

I stared at Jenny's slender fingers where they intertwined with mine. Her skin was so soft and fair, next to my swarthy tanned hands. She looked so delicate, but she wasn't.

She was unbelievably strong.

I knew, because I had just watched her give birth.

Yep. I was a daddy. Again.

This time, though, I got to see the birth. I got to be there, holding my woman's hand, cheering her on. And I would never forget it as long as I lived.

The miracle of birth was messy. Scary. Agonizing at times.

And the most amazing, miraculous thing that I'd seen in my entire life. My woman had made this perfect human being with her body. I'd just added one little ingredient.

She'd done all the hard work.

That was my Jenny, the hardest worker in the whole damn world.

The nurse came over and handed the baby to Jenny. I scooted my chair even closer, watching as she pulled the blanket back to look at our sweet girl's face.

That's right. The irony was not lost on me. Sergeant Panty Dropper was now the proud daddy of two little girls.

Two beauties, just like their mama.

Now there were three under one roof. Basically, my house was the center of whole damn universe. Where pretty ladies were concerned anyway.

Pretty, smart, strong, amazing, brilliant, wonderful women.

And I had three of them.

I'd spend the rest of my life protecting them and loving all three of them. Even if that meant I had to chase hundreds of boys away. I was happy to do the job.

I was *privileged* to do it.

I didn't know how the hell I got to be so damn lucky.

"Can I hold her?"

Jenny smiled softly and I opened my arms, cradling my little girl against my chest. Hallie was back home. The General and his new girlfriend were watching her. He'd actually started dating one of the women I'd brought to the wedding.

My plan had backfired. The old bastard was happier than a pig in shit. And he was over the moon about his new granddaughter, chomping at the bit to get over here and meet her.

I'd just have to think of something new to get to him.

Maybe something to do with diaper duty...

I grinned and smiled down at my wife.

"Catherine?"

She nodded. We'd talked about naming the little girl after her mother. And now we had. Jenny cleared her throat.

"Catherine Susan Jagger."

I stared at her, love shining in my eyes. After everything, after she'd thought Suze was someone who I'd turned to when we broke up, she'd embraced my wild little foster sister. In fact, she was on her way here to stay with us for a couple of weeks. She couldn't wait to help with the baby.

And now my beautiful wife had named her after the one bit of family I had. It could not have been more perfect. She was the light of my life, and that was the damn truth.

"You're amazing, wife."

"You're not bad yourself, husband."

I threw back my head and laughed, accidentally waking the baby. Catherine Susan Jagger started to cry. She had a set of lungs on her like you wouldn't believe.

I grinned and winked at my wife.

"Especially not my hair."

She rolled her eyes.

"And definitely not my taste in women."

She leaned back and I nestled the baby into her arms. They were both getting sleepy and Cathy needed to feed. I sat back and watched as Jenny breastfed our little girl for the first time.

She looked so peaceful. So lovely and relaxed and complete. It was a good thing she had no idea what was running through my mind.

I couldn't stop thinking about getting to work on number three.

NOTE FROM THE AUTHOR

Thank you for reading *Cockpit!* If you enjoyed this book please let me know by reviewing where you bought the book and on <u>Goodreads</u>! You can find me on <u>Facebook</u>, <u>Twitter</u>, or you can email me at: <u>JoannaBlakeRomance@gmail.com</u>

Credits:

    LJ Anderson, Mayhem Cover Design
    James Critchley, Cover Photo
    Andrew England, Cover Model
    Just One More Page Book Promotions
    Pincushion Press

Other works by <u>Joanna Blake</u>:

    BRO'
    A Bad Boy For Summer
    PLAYER
    GRIND
    HEAT
    PUSH
    DEEP
    Go Long
    Go Big

Turn the page for excerpts from Joanna Blake's _PLAYER_, _Go Long_ and _Stud Farm_ (*The Delancey Brother's Trilogy*)

ALSO BY JOANNA BLAKE

PLAYER

JAMES

"Yo' Fitz! Your turn man."

I looked up to see Kyle grinning stupidly as the stripper finished grinding on him. The song was ending and Kyle had his hands all over the dancer's generous ass. The girl, Crystal something or other, was only wearing a G-string. Her tanned skin gleamed in the dim light.

I drank deeply from my twenty-dollar beer. Thankfully drinks were free for the team. As were the lap dances. And anything else that might arise.

Players frequently went home with the dancers from the club. I had myself more than once. The girls were severely hot and more than accommodating. Not to mention flexible.

I shook my head. To be honest, I felt kind of disgusting the last time I woke up next to a girl whose makeup was smeared all over the pillow case. And the sheets. And my cock. When I was drunk, then yeah, I didn't mind so much. But after...

Lately all the girls I boned made me feel that way. The strippers, the groupies, the coeds. I'd even picked up a housewife at a bar just a week ago. Well, to be honest. She'd picked me up.

But something about it was leaving me unsatisfied.

More than unsatisfied.

I felt fucking dirty.

If I was honest, I preferred the natural look. Like that gorgeous brunette in my economy class. She might be a freshman, but she had all the right equipment. Huge green eyes, a cute nose, gorgeous lips, and the best tits I'd seen in my entire life.

My God those tits could stop traffic. Not to mention her legs were about a mile long. They'd look nice wrapped around me as I drove in and out of her sweet little box.

I adjusted my junk. I was hard just thinking about it.

The dancer walked towards me with a question in her eyes.

"I'll pass."

I wasn't drunk enough to enjoy this tonight. Even after winning yet another game. I should be riding high but instead I just wanted to be alone.

The thing was, I was hardly fucking ever alone.

My teammates, the fans, girls. I was the center of attention. Non-stop.

Growing up, I'd had the opposite problem. My mom had worked two jobs. Sometimes three. And we'd still been dirt poor.

Fuck, poorer than that.

Mud poor.

If you'd ever seen the neighborhood I grew up in, it was probably on the news. Some reporter talking about crime rates. Or how depressed the south side of Chicago was. And how everyone who lived there was either a vandal or a hoodlum.

Or both.

I'd like to say that I hadn't been one of those criminals but that would be a lie. I'd jacked car stereos, bikes, anything. The only thing that had saved me from ending up in prison was football.

The Sport of Kings.

Look at me now. I was the top of the heap. The King of Kings.

And I was still fucking covered in mud.

ALSO BY JOANNA BLAKE

GRIND

CHAN

Something wet slid against my ear. I brushed it away, still half asleep. It grazed my skin again and I rolled away from it. I tried to wipe it off on the pillow beneath my head, grimacing at the slimy sensation. Now I was awake and I didn't want to be.

Damn.

I opened my eyes to see a woman bending over me. Her long blond hair brushed my face. I turned my head away.

"Cut it out."

She sat up, glaring at me.

"You didn't seem to mind last night."

Normally, I would have soothed her. Called her by name. Trouble is, I had no fucking clue who the hell she was.

I looked around.

I had no idea *where* I was either.

"Fuck me."

She grinned at me, tossing that long bleached hair over her shoulder.

"I already did."

Belatedly I noticed that she was wearing some serious lingerie. Black and cream lace.

It matched her bedroom. Her very expensive looking bedroom.

I was swimming in a sea of neutral toned sheets and blankets. Silk probably. Expensive, definitely.

"I'd like to again."

I shook my head.

"Sorry babe, I gotta go."

She pouted. I rolled out of bed, looking for my clothes.

"Oh come on... Didn't we have fun together last night?"

I smiled and nodded. It's not that she was bad looking, even if she was at least a decade older than me. It was hard to tell with these rich older broads. She was toned, buffed and polished to a high shine.

Well preserved didn't even begin to cover it.

Yeah, she was hot. Not just for a cougar. But I wasn't in the mood. I didn't usually go for seconds anyway.

Hell. I never did.

Hit it and quit it was my motto. It served me well. I didn't want any entanglements and I doubted I ever would.

I looked at her, giving my best impersonation of someone who gave a shit.

"Where are my clothes?"

She smiled back and shrugged.

"I really couldn't say."

Fucking hell.

"That's great. Just great."

I looked around the room, lifting cushions and opening drawers. Nada. On the bedside table were my keys, wallet and phone. I scooped them up, thanking God for small favors.

"Have a nice day, Ma'am."

"Wait- you aren't leaving like that!"

I coyly waved bye bye to her and left. I jogged through her palatial house in the buff. The marble floors were cool under my feet. The place screamed mega bucks. But not in a tacky way. It was tastefully done, just like the lady herself.

She was chasing me through the house, becoming less composed by the second.

"Seriously, you can't! What will the neighbors think?"

I stopped at the front door of her mansion, glancing back over my shoulder.

"You should have thought of that before you hid my shit."

She screamed in frustration and threw a vase at me. I heard it shatter against the door as I closed it behind me. Just in the nick of time.

"Damn. That would have left a mark."

I made a call as I strolled down her manicured driveway to the gate.

"Joss, can you pick me up? I need a ride."

I leaned against the wrought iron gate and waved at a neighbor who was walking their dog.

"Take your time."

ALSO BY JOANNA BLAKE

GO LONG

BELINDA

"How do you like our campus so far Kyle?"

Kyle smiled benignly at my mother. He looked as innocent as a choirboy. Meanwhile, under the table his foot was brushing mine. I wasn't sure if it was deliberate until he did it again. I scowled at him as he oozed charm and good will. All false of course.

I wasn't fooled.

"It's the most beautiful I've ever seen. And the students have been... very friendly."

He grinned at me pointedly and popped a bite of food into his mouth. He made it clear he was talking about me as his foot caressed mine again. I kicked him and he nearly choked. I smiled serenely as my father pounded his back.

Kyle glared at me as he wiped his mouth.

I gave him a look that clearly said 'two can play at that game.'

"Thank you Coach."

"Make sure you chew your food, boy. Can't lose you before the season starts!"

I put my chin on my hand and smiled sweetly. I knew more about sports than most men. But Kyle didn't know that. I intended to milk it.

"Daddy, isn't it unusual to put a walk-on on the team?"

"Hardly ever happens at this level. But Kyle here is an unusual young man."

"He is?"

"He's unnaturally talented on the field Bellie. His military training had a lot to do with it, but some people are just naturals."

"Bellie?"

Kyle's eyes were glowing mischievously. I could have screamed. My plan to control the conversation had completely backfired. If he started calling me 'Bellie' I would lose it. I really would.

"That's what we call our little girl. Did you know they actually pay her to attend school? She had a full ride of course, but they actually give her a stipend and all sorts of administrative jobs for extra money. She has career academic written all over her."

I groaned inwardly. Did he have to make me sound like a cross between a 12 year-old and a grandma? That's what I was really. Kyle was right when he called me Miss Priss. Just a little girl who acted like the biggest, most responsible, boring goodie two-shoes ever to walk the face of the-

Kyle was staring at my breasts. Not just staring either. He licked his lips and made an appreciative grimace. Like he couldn't stand being this close to me and not touching me.

I coughed, nearly spitting out my mashed potatoes.

He was touching me with his eyes. It was practically foreplay! I tried to ignore him but it was too late. A hot pool of lust had settled in my belly. I crossed my arms, realizing my nipples were hard. I jumped up, knocking over my glass of iced tea.

Thankfully it was almost empty.

"Bellie! Are you alright?"

"Just- chilly. I want to grab a sweater."

"Alright but come right back and we can clear the table."

"Yes, mom."

I practically ran from the room. I could feel Kyle's eyes boring into my back. I heard him ask where the restroom was and excuse himself.

Argh!!! He was following me!

I ran for my bedroom and started to slam the door but he caught it with the flat of his hand.

"Where are you running to... Bellie?"

He was grinning at me like the cat that ate the canary. I had the sudden urge to smack the smug look off his handsome face. His eyes slid over my body, even more blatantly than before. I grabbed a light cardigan, angrily pulling it over my arms. I buttoned the center of it.

"Don't call me that!"

He just shook his head, leaning against my doorframe.

"Why not? You know I can still see those perfect tits of your, Bellie. Your nipples are practically poking a hole through that sweater."

I gasped.

"My father will hear you!"

He grinned.

"No. He won't."

He stepped into my room and I stepped backwards until my back was against the wall. He loomed over me, saying nothing.

Then he ran his hands over my shoulders, deliberately brushing my breasts with his forearms.

"Did I do that to you, Miss Priss?"

I opened my mouth but no words came out. He was making me confused dammit! And he *had* done this to me... without even touching me, I was aroused like never before.

Well, like only *once* before anyway.

"Meet me tomorrow after practice at my dorm. Unless you want me to tell him what you've been up to."

I glared at him.

"Blackmail? Really?"

He nodded slowly.

"I will stoop to anything to get what I want, Bellie. What we both want."

I inhaled sharply as he leaned forward, his lips brushing my ear. I closed my eyes, feeling my heart thud in my chest. My whole body felt alive. I could feel the heat rolling off him. The strength. I could smell that clean manly scent... images of our night together flooded my mind against my will. I whimpered, ready to fall into his arms. All he had to do was kiss me.

But he didn't. He just breathed four soft words against my ear, sending shivers down my spine. At that moment, even my goosebumps had goosebumps.

"And I want you."

When I opened my eyes, he was gone.

ALSO BY JOANNA BLAKE

STUD FARM

The Delancey Brothers

DANIEL

I pushed Black Jack to his limits, riding the stallion over the entire course. I did this nearly every morning now before his afternoon training session. Ever since the wild young horse had arrived.

It kept him from injuring himself or the trainers.

I was the only one the damned horse would listen to.

I rode into the paddock and dismounted, tossing the reins to McDermott, the head stable master.

"Your appointment is waiting for you Daniel."

He winked at me.

"What appointment?"

"She was supposed to be here last week, remember?"

I cursed. A rich city girl was here to breed her horse with one of ours. She'd been carefully instructed that the sooner in the mare's season she came, the better the chances that the mare would quicken.

But the prearranged date had come and gone without a word.

I'd had the staff call. I'd emailed. And then I'd written it off.

I was inclined to ignore the matter entirely. Just to teach the lady a lesson in manners. Leave the horse unbred.

But I couldn't.

Jackson had personally tasked me with this client.

Damnit.

"Personally, I'd say she was worth the wait."

I glanced at McDermott sardonically.

"The mare or the woman?"

He chuckled.

"Both!"

I smiled at his joke and patted Black Jack's flank.

"Cool him down and clean him off. It's time for him to meet his first girlfriend."

"What about you?"

He gestured to my riding clothes. I'd been out for hours, sweating in the Texas sun. I looked down at myself.

I pulled out a handkerchief and wiped my face.

"That's as good as the lady is going to get. Where is she?"

"Where else? The stables."

I nodded. Where else, indeed.

Horse people were all the same. Even if they were God awful in human company. But each and every one loved the majestic animals with an intense fervor unmatched by other hobbyists.

I strode into the massive stable building, eager to get this over with. The stables were L-shaped. She wasn't in the first corridor so I turned the corner.

And stopped in my tracks.

Leaning against one of the stable doors was a tall, slender, very, very curvy woman. Her long blond hair was artfully arranged in luxurious waves. Her outrageously perfect bottom was encased in snug fitting riding pants. Her profile was one of classic beauty, with thickly lashed eyes, high cheekbones, a delicate nose and pouty lips.

Did I mention the curves?

Her entire bearing screamed old money, privilege and pride.

And stupidity.

She was leaning against Thunderstorm's stall. The one horse who'd been known to injure anyone who rode him. Or got close to his stall. The most dangerous horse in a hundred miles.

"Back away very slowly."

Her head turned and she stared at me. Her eyes were wide as she took me in. For a moment she looked pleasantly surprised. And then disdain clouded her features. She looked me up and down, obviously confusing me for a stable hand.

I'd been wrong.

The woman wasn't just a beauty.

She was *the beauty*.

The most beautiful woman I'd ever laid eyes on.

I had one question answered.

Her eyes were blue.

And I knew one other thing for certain too.

She was about to become a major pain in my ass.

Made in the USA
Middletown, DE
27 December 2018